EDGE OF REALITY

THE UPHEAVAL BOOK 2

CHARLEY MARSH

Timberdoodle Press

Edge of Reality

Copyright © 2018 by Charley Marsh

All rights reserved.

Published 2018 by Timberdoodle Press.

Edge of Reality is a work of fiction. The characters, incidents, and places are the product of the author's imagination or are used fictitiously. Any resemblance to actual events, locales, or persons living or dead is entirely coincidental.

No part of this book may be reproduced in any form or by any electronic or mechanical means, including information storage and retrieval systems, without written permission from the author, except for the use of brief quotations in a book review. For more information contact the publisher: http://timberdoodlepress.com/

All rights reserved

E-Book ISBN# 978-1-945856-04-4

Print Book ISBN# 978-1-945856-39-6

Cover Art: depositphoto.com and Kessler Photo

"WHAT HAPPENED TO NEBRASKA?"

Sydney Waters stood at the edge of the steep precipice and glared at the desert plain below. It stretched as far as she could see until it faded into the distant gray horizon. She tried to hold her annoyance and frustration in check. This next leg of their journey should have been easy, but Mother Earth had thrown her a curveball.

Her original plan had been to walk straight west across South Dakota and into Wyoming, but a near run-in with a band of travelers had forced them to veer south into Nebraska. After their experience in Driftwood, Sydney intended to avoid all people, even if it meant walking extra miles.

She sighed and turned to her companion. "I don't get it. Nebraska should be flat and green. Instead it looks like a sunken desert."

Jordan James turned his sightless gray eyes toward Sydney and shrugged one shoulder.

"My sister believed the upheaval was the earth's way of filling in all the voids man created. She told me that we pumped too much oil and water out of the planet and dug too many mines. I used to tease her and call her an environmental alarmist."

A tightness crossed his face, there and gone so swiftly Sydney would have missed it if she hadn't been standing so near. She laid a hand on Jordan's arm and squeezed gently. She knew he still ached with the pain of his sister's untimely death.

Torrie James had died from lack of medical care two months earlier. A simple cut from a rusted piece of farm machinery had led to septicemia, a deadly infection if left untreated as Torrie's had been.

"The Ogallala Aquifer sits underneath several of the plains states, including most of Nebraska. If the land has sunk, I'd say Torrie's theory was right. The aquifer was pumped dry and the land above it has dropped."

Sydney scowled. Several months ago her goal had seemed so simple: find her friend Smokey. But there had been nothing but problems since she had left her family farm on the banks of the Mississippi River.

First Jordan had locked her in his storm cellar until she agreed to help him. She didn't blame him for that, he had been slowly starving to death without his sister's care. It wasn't easy for a blind man to find food in the new world. Heck, it wasn't easy for anyone to find enough to eat.

Unwilling to leave Jordan behind, Sydney had brought him along with her, hoping to find someone to care for him.

Then they had walked into Driftwood, South Dakota and stumbled into a nest of escaped convicts.

Now they were facing a great desert that shouldn't exist.

"I had planned to head due west across Nebraska, but without water we won't get far," she said. "We'll have to follow this ridge south until we get beyond the aquifer.

Besides, this cliff is too steep to safely descend even if we wanted to cross the desert."

She reached down and absently scratched between Dogma's ears, the thick fur rough and wiry under Sydney's fingers. The giant dog pressed her head against Sydney's hip for a moment and gazed across the land below them.

Sydney wondered what she thought about their situation. She wished Dogma could speak; she was open to any suggestions at this point, and Dogma was an intelligent dog.

"Watch out, Jordan, you're awfully close to the edge. There are cracks in the dirt—the cliff could crumble away beneath you."

Her warning came a moment too late. Jordan yelled as the edge of the cliff broke away and he disappeared from sight.

Sydney dropped to her belly and inched forward until she could see down the cliff face. She watched Jordan roll and tumble to the bottom of the cliff and come to an abrupt stop in the pale dirt.

"Jordan? Jordan! Are you all right?" There was no answer and no sign of movement from Jordan. Dread filled her. What if he was dead? She should've been paying closer attention. Sometimes she forgot that her companion was a blind man.

"Crap! Come on, Dogma, we have to get down there. Jordan needs us!"

The massive dog whined, then edged her feet carefully over the cliff edge. She flattened her belly and slid over the edge and began to pick her way down the steep slope before she lost her balance and slid to the bottom on her hind quarters.

To Sydney's relief, Dogma bounced to her feet and trotted over to where Jordan lay.

Watching Dogma's awkward descent gave Sydney an

idea. She sat on the edge of the cliff and extended her legs. Leaning back, she dug the bottom edge of her backpack into the dirt to act as a brake. The two hens, confined to twin cages made of thin woven branches, squawked as their cages swung from the top of the pack and hit the dirt.

"Don't worry, girls. I won't let anything happen to you. I'm going to try to do this in a more controlled and elegant manner than Jordan did. Ready?"

Sydney scooted off the edge of the cliff and began to slide downward, her legs stiff in front of her body and her arms spread wide. She dug her heels and hands into the slope as she slid down, trying to slow her speed.

The hillside was steeper than she realized and for a moment she regretted her decision to follow Jordan.

Dirt worked its way into her pant legs and boots and up her back, but at least she stayed upright. She reached out and grabbed Jordan's staff as she slid by the spot where he dropped it. Moments later she safely reached the bottom of the slope.

Sydney scrambled to her feet and pulled off her pack. She removed Ginny and Harriet's cages and set the hens aside, then hurried over to where Jordan lay.

His face looked pale under his tan, but she found a pulse and was relieved to see that he seemed to be breathing okay.

She knelt beside him and carefully felt for broken bones. She ran her hands over Jordan's strong, muscled thighs, glad that he was unconscious so he could not see the way touching him flustered her.

Sydney forced her attention back to the problem at hand. As soon as she was sure no bones were broken she put her hand on Jordan's shoulder and gently shook him.

"Jordan? Jordan! Wake up!"

Jordan groaned. His eyes fluttered open and closed again. Blood ran from a gash over one eye.

"Don't move yet, okay? I don't think anything is broken but you have a nasty cut on your face." Sydney dug into Jordan's pack and pulled out a strip of bed sheet.

"We'll have to thank the Doc for giving us these makeshift bandages when we see her again," she said as she wet one end of the sheet strip with a small amount of their precious water and dabbed at the wound on Jordan's head. She added a few drops of iodine to the cloth and dabbed again.

Doc Melody had not had much iodine to spare so Spencer was very careful with their woefully tiny supply.

Jordan jerked away from her touch. "Ow, not so hard. Sadist. Where'd you learn your bedside manners anyway? Whatever happened to kiss and make it better?" he grumbled.

Sydney smiled. The head wound couldn't be too serious if Jordan felt well enough to complain.

"Don't be such a wuss," she scolded. "Hold still until I get this wound cleaned up and bandaged."

She finished wiping the blood off Jordan's face and wrapped the makeshift bandage around his head, tying the ends off neatly the way Doc Melody had taught her.

Ten long minutes passed before Jordan felt able to sit up. He rolled his shoulders and neck experimentally. "Holy cow, that was an unexpected ride. I take it we are now in the sunken desert?"

"Yeah. I'm afraid there's no way we can climb back up that cliff, it's practically vertical. You're lucky you didn't break your neck."

Jordan scowled. Once again he had made life much more difficult for Sydney. Being blind was a real pain in his ass.

He'd like to take care of her for a change, but it was hard to be the strong one when he couldn't see the danger.

"Tell me what you see," he said.

Sydney shrugged, then for the thousandth time remembered Jordan couldn't see the gesture. Most of the time he didn't act blind and she forgot that he couldn't see. And then things like falling off cliffs happen, she thought with a scowl.

"I can't see much," she said. "We're standing at the bottom of a cliff that I guesstimate is around one hundred fifty to two hundred feet high. There's nothing but flat land in the other three directions. No buildings, no sign of a town or a city, and no green anywhere."

She helped Jordan to his feet, handed him his carved ironwood staff, and checked his pack. Fortunately she carried their cooking pots or Jordan would have sustained some nasty bruising when he fell. The clothes and bedding in his pack had helped absorb some of the impact as he tumbled.

When she felt satisfied that all was secure, she retied the hen's cages to the top of her own pack and put it back on.

"We're stuck down here now. I think we should head south. We'll travel along the base of the cliff and maybe find a way to climb back up. Keep your fingers crossed we find water soon. We have enough for the two of us for a day or so, but Dogma will need a fresh source before then."

Jordan swayed slightly on his feet. "I'm still a little woozy. Must be from somersaulting down the cliff. I swear I felt my brain sloshing around inside my skull a few times."

"Can you tell which way is south?" Sydney tried to keep her concern out of her voice. She suspected Jordan had suffered a mild concussion during his fall, but she didn't want to alarm him with her worries.

Jordan lifted his face to the sun and spun in a slow circle.

"It's after noon, so the sun is moving to the west." He stopped with the sun on his right and pointed straight ahead. "That way is south."

"I'm impressed." A little of the tension eased from Sydney's shoulders. Jordan's fall made her painfully aware of their vulnerability to injury. Neither of them had medical experience and they carried only the most basic of supplies. They would have to be more careful. An unset broken bone, or even a simple cut, could mean infection and a slow, painful death.

"I think we should travel a little away from the bottom of the cliff to avoid any falling rocks," she said, eyeing a few boulders that had obviously rolled down the cliff face.

Dogma took her usual place, pressed close to Jordan's thigh, and they set off, an unusual group of travelers in the strange, alien-scape of a sunken giant aquifer.

Sydney led the way through crisp dead grasses and shriveled shrubbery. Dry cracked earth, reminding her of crackleur on old pottery, was all that remained of once green crop and hay fields. Leafless gray-trunked trees loomed over them like ghostly skeletons. The baked dirt reflected the sun's rays and intensified the searing heat.

By the time the sun swung low to the west, they were a bedraggled and sorry looking group. Dogma's long, pink tongue hung from her slack, panting mouth. Sydney's shirt clung to her back, plastered there by her dried sweat. The hens had stopped their constant clucking and were unusually silent, their small beaks parted and feathers fluffed as they tried to release the punishing heat from their bodies.

Sydney stopped and scanned the land before them. They

needed a safe spot to spend the night. If she were alone she would continue to travel through the cooler temperatures of darkness, but she sensed Jordan's fatigue. His steps had become stiff and wooden, and his usually straight, broad shoulders slumped. She couldn't push any further until they'd all rested.

She looked without much hope for a stand of green or any sign of surface water, but only shades of brown and gray colored the landscape. She pulled out her binoculars and searched for an overhang or indentation in the cliff—anything that would offer them shelter, no matter how slight.

Sydney spied a jumble of rocks at the base of the cliff and altered course for them. The rock's shadows would provide some welcome relief from the relentless sun, and maybe even protection from any hungry beasts of prey that might be prowling the desert for a meal.

She touched the crossbow pistol hanging from her pack and patted the quiver of bolts tied to her thigh. In her concern for Jordan she had forgotten about them. It was fortunate that she hadn't lost them during her descent.

She berated herself for being so careless. That sort of forgetfulness could cost them their lives.

The crossbow was not only her main means of hunting food, it was their only protection. Doc Melody had offered her a pistol and ammunition but they were heavy to carry, and the pistol would be useless once the ammunition ran out.

Spencer would rather rely on the weapon she knew best, plus she could always fashion new bolts for the crossbow, a great advantage over the pistol.

Fifteen minutes later they reached the pile of large, flat slabs of rock. A distinct scar two-thirds up the cliff identified the source of the fallen rocks. They had sheared off from the cliff face, perhaps during the cataclysm that caused the land's surface to sink to its current position.

Sydney felt grateful for the rock fall regardless of when it had happened. She removed her pack with a soft groan and set the hen cages in the shade beneath a tilted gray monolith of stone. She dug a water bottle from her pack and offered it to Jordan.

Jordan drank only enough of the unpleasantly warm water to ease the dryness of his mouth and throat and handed the bottle back. They both knew they needed to conserve what little water they carried until they could find a source to replenish it. Lack of water was now their greatest foe, far more worrisome than lack of food or even wild beasts.

Sydney took a small sip and filled the cap. She offered the water to each hen, then poured a small amount into one of their cooking pots for Dogma. The dog lapped the pot dry and licked Sydney's hand. She swore she saw gratitude in Dogma's golden eyes and made her a silent promise to find her fresh water soon.

After a brief rest Sydney climbed to the top of a flat gray slab with her binoculars in hand. She searched for any sign of people or life in the desert landscape. There was still no a hint of green to be found and no sign of civilization. The newly formed desert stretched before her until it disappeared in a gray haze.

She spun and turned the binoculars toward the south and saw nothing but towering cliff walls fading into the distance. Same to the north. There was no way to climb out of the sunken aquifer. They were stuck in this strange desolate desert land.

Dejected by what they faced, Sydney carefully climbed down off the boulder. They had an unknown distance to go and enough water for one more day. Their situation had become desperate. They needed a miracle or they would perish.

"Jordan, I need to take care of some personal business on the other side of this rock field. I'll be back in a few minutes."

Jordan waved two fingers at her from his seat in the shade of a broad slab. His dirt-streaked face shone bright red against the white bandage. "Take Dogma with you just in case there are wild animals hanging around. I can't believe anything besides snakes lives in this dirt furnace, but you never know."

Sydney circled the boulder field with Dogma at her heels. Some of the rocks were significantly taller than her diminutive five foot five inches. They were steep-sided, impossible to climb. A jumbled pile of narrow, flat slabs reminded her of a barn she had once seen after it had been hit by a tornado and the barn boards rearranged into an unrecognizable mess.

She saw no sign of life, not even the small lizards that one might find living in the southern deserts.

If there was any life in the desert it was waiting for night-fall to move. They would be wise to do the same if they wanted any chance to survive.

The thought came unbidden but she knew it was the truth. They would rest until sunset and then move on, she decided.

Sydney rounded the last of the boulders and stared at the base of the steep slope. Dead ahead of her stood the dark mouth of a cave. Beside her, Dogma's ears pricked forward and her body grew rigid.

Sydney tensed and waited but nothing happened. She curled her hand in Dogma's thick ruff. "What do you think, girl? Should we check it out?"

Dogma wagged her long tail and gave a soft woof.

"Okay, then. Let's go see if it's safe. It will be cooler to rest inside a cave than under those hot rocks." Sydney moved forward, never taking her eyes off the cave's entrance. Three steps, stop and wait. Repeat.

Without thinking, she had slid into the Slow Walk that her friend Smokey had taught her for navigating unseen through the forest. Movement caught the hunter's eye. Minimize movement to avoid detection. It was a lesson that all successful prey animals learned.

Sydney had learned the hard way that humans occupied both niches: predator and prey.

When she reached the outer edge of the cave's mouth, she stopped again to listen. A faint whiff of moisture hung in the cave's entrance. Even more exciting, she thought she heard the drip of water coming from deep inside the cave.

Beside her, Dogma leaned toward the scent of water and whined. Her nose quivered and she took a step into the cave.

Sydney knew that Dogma would be on alert if she sensed any danger. She released her hold on Dogma's ruff. "Okay, girl, go ahead. I know you're thirsty. I'll follow you."

She ducked through the cave's mouth and immediately found herself in a large, open cavern. The cave floor felt smooth and dry and firm under her feet. The ceiling soared somewhere out of sight, lost in darkness. Goosebumps raised on her arms as she entered the cooler air.

The cave smelled of water, moist earth, minerals, and slightly stale air. The lack of bat guano surprised her until she remembered that bats require enormous quantities of insects to survive and there were few, if any, living in the desert outside the cave.

The light from the cave's entrance grew dimmer as she followed Dogma deeper into the cave toward the sound of dripping water. She still could not see the roof of the cavern, but she sensed that it had sloped downward and now hung closer overhead.

Sydney shivered and wrapped her arms around her chest to ward off the chill. It felt delicious after the searing heat of the day.

The light from the cave's mouth dwindled to a faint dusk. Sydney closed her eyes and then reopened them to help them adjust to the semi-dark. Just ahead, a faint reflection from the floor of the cave told her she had found the source of the dripping water.

Dogma walked into the pool and greedily lapped it up, then laid down in the shallow water with a happy-dog groan. She climbed out of the water after a few moments, shook herself vigorously and sat on the cave floor.

Sydney estimated the pool to be about thirty feet across. Was it clean enough to drink without boiling? she wondered. She hesitated, then knelt, cupped one hand, and sampled the water. It tasted of minerals, sharp and a little bitter.

She cupped both hands and took a big drink, letting the water flow between her fingers and down her neck and chest. The water felt cold and bracing, almost frigid. She sat back and waited for the pool's surface to grow calm.

Drip. Small ripples spread across the pool. Sydney let her focus soften and broaden as she watched the pool.

Drip. This time she saw the droplet fall. The pool water was either from condensation dripping from the ceiling of the cave, or a water source flowed above the cave and some of it had forced its way through the rock.

Sydney stood and turned to leave but stopped short. A frisson of fear went through her. A trail of muddy footprints headed from the pool deeper into the cave. She tried to peer into the dark recesses of the cave, afraid she was being observed by some possibly dangerous person, but then remembered Dogma. Dogma would've let her know if they had company.

Relieved, she bent down and inspected the faint prints, wishing she had a flashlight to help her see. Unfortunately battery-powered equipment was a thing of the past.

There was light enough to see that the prints were made by bare feet and were all the same size. There seemed to be a steady track of them. They created a light brown path on the darker cave floor. Someone either lived in the cave, or there was another route through the cave to the pond.

Sydney straightened and mulled over her discovery. She hadn't noticed any prints coming into the cave, or traveling from the cave mouth to the pool.

That meant that others used the cave and accessed it through another entrance. Perhaps that entrance could lead them out of the desert and back up onto higher, greener land.

Sydney hurried back toward the mouth of the cave with Dogma close behind. She needed to fetch Jordan. Traveling through a dark cave would be a cakewalk for a blind man.

2

"JORDAN! Get up. I found a cave and water and maybe a way out of this awful place." Sydney grabbed the hen's cages and tied them onto her pack. She slipped into it and grabbed Jordan's pack.

"C'mon, it's much cooler in the cave. Take my hand." She reached down and tried to pull Jordan to his feet.

"You found a cave in the cliff?" Jordan's brain felt fuzzy. He was having trouble thinking clearly and it scared him. He wondered if he was suffering from sunstroke or heatstroke. After the car accident that had cost him his sight he had rarely ventured outdoors. There were too many unknowns and too many ways for a blind man to come to harm.

With the earth's violent upheaval his life as a world renowned entertainer had come to an abrupt end. People were consumed with the fight to stay alive and there was no longer any call for a piano man, even one as talented and popular as he had been. He had holed up with his sister on their parent's farm, until Torrie died and Sydney had come along and rescued him from certain death by starvation.

She had forced him out of the house he was born and

raised in, out of his comfort zone, away from everything that felt familiar, and taken him on a horizon expanding adventure. His thoughts drifted to the first time he had kissed her at Doc Melody's house. She tasted so sweet and…

"Piano Man! Pay attention here." Sydney squinted at her companion. "Are you all right? Your eyes look a little glazed." She placed the back of her hand on his face. "You're burning up. We need to get you out of this heat pronto. Get up."

Jordan wished she hadn't taken her hand away from his face. It felt cool and soothing and soft and smooth. What did she want him to do? Oh yeah, gotta move…He crawled to his feet awkwardly.

Sydney grabbed his hand again and pulled him after her, juggling his pack and staff in her other hand.

He stumbled, embarrassed by his sudden clumsiness and his weakened state. A man was supposed to take care of his woman, not the other way around. And Sydney was his woman, he felt very sure of that.

She might not know it yet, but they belonged together. He would make that very clear to this Smokey guy when they found him. No matter what prior claims Smokey thought he had on Sydney, she belonged to Jordan now.

"Duck down, Jordan. A little more. That's it. We're entering the cave now. Feel the cooler air?" Sydney led Jordan several steps inside and then dropped his hand. She set down his belongings and her pack and grabbed the hen's cages. Dogma pressed against Jordan's leg.

"Hold onto Dogma, Jordan. I'm taking you to the water. We'll get your body temp down in a few minutes. It should make you feel better." Sydney set the hens down beside the pool and let them out of their cages. They made their way to the water and drank, then started scratching around the cave floor. She hoped they could find some bugs in the cave as she had no food left to feed them.

"Sit here, I need to check your wound." She led Jordan to the edge of the water and put his free hand into it.

He bent down and plunged his head into the water, then drank straight from the pool. Despite the metallic flavor he thought it might be the best water he'd ever tasted.

He sat quietly while Sydney checked his wound and replaced the bandage with a dry one, enjoying the closeness of her warm body and her gentle touch. He breathed in her unique scent, trying not to be obvious about it. She smelled wonderful, like spice and sweet green plants and something he thought might be essence of female, if there was such a thing.

"I think we'd better rest here tonight, then we'll look for the other entrance," said Sydney. "I'll go fetch our packs and be back in a jiffy. Don't go away." She squeezed his shoulder and left.

Jordan listened to the sound of her steps moving off, heard her pick up their packs, and followed the sound of her return.

He might be blind, he mused, but his awareness of the things around him had grown since he started this journey with Sydney. He had more to be grateful to her for than just his life.

He breathed in the sharp tang of minerals and water and grimaced at the smell of sour sweat emanating from his body. He would've known they were inside a cave even without Sydney telling him. His ears told him he was in an enclosed space. It was a large space, but confined. He could sense the walls, and somehow knew they weren't close by.

The cold water and cooler interior of the cave lessened

the stress of heat on his brain and body. He breathed a sigh of relief. He felt sharper, more in control.

"Did you say there are footprints leading away from here?" he asked Sydney as she drew close.

"Yes, they're on the opposite side of this pool. They head directly away from the cave's mouth. I think there has to be another entrance."

Sydney set down the packs and placed the staff next to Jordan. She pulled the last of their jerky from her pack and split it, handing Jordan half. She gave half of her portion to Dogma who took it gently from her fingers.

"This is the last of the jerky. No eggs from Ginny and Harriet today, I'm afraid. They haven't been getting enough to eat to lay any for us."

They ate in silence. They both knew that they needed to get back to land where Sydney could find food before she became to weak to hunt and forage.

"I'm sorry," Jordan said, after he'd finished his portion of the jerky.

"For what? You haven't done anything to apologize for."

"If I hadn't fallen down the cliff face you'd be able to hunt for food and we wouldn't be in this mess."

"It wasn't your fault, Jordan. It was an accident. How could you know the cliff edge would crumble out from underneath you? I'm supposed to be looking out for you. If it's anyone's fault, it's mine."

Jordan scowled. "I don't need you feeling responsible for me. That's not how it's supposed to be." Her words made him feel angry and frustrated. He hated that Sydney felt responsible for him. He should be looking out for her.

Sydney misinterpreted Jordan's scowl. At times Jordan's unwillingness to admit he was handicapped irritated her, at others she felt proud of his efforts at independence. It wasn't a subject they'd been able to talk about—yet.

"Anyway, I found water, didn't I?" She said aloud. "Don't worry, we'll find a way out of here. You'll have to lead the way when we head deeper into the cave. Your ability to sense objects will come in handy. Once we leave the light from the cave entrance I won't be able to see a thing. I'll be blinder than you."

Jordan's foul mood disappeared. A small smile lifted one corner of his mouth. "That will be a change. A real case of the blind leading the blind, wouldn't you say?"

Sydney set out their sleeping bags, and they soon fell asleep, leaving Dogma on guard.

Before they left the pool, Sydney filled their water bottles and they drank as much as their stomachs could hold. She placed Ginny and Harriet in their cages, promising the mahogany-colored hens that she would find them some bugs or fresh greens soon.

When all was ready she led Jordan to the far side of the pool and aligned him with the footprints. "They head in this direction." She lifted his arm and pointed along the muddy path.

Jordan took a deep breath and let it out. "All right then. Let's see if a blind man can find his way through a dark cave." He started forward with Dogma at his side and Sydney close on his heels.

Within minutes they lost the last of the light from the cave's mouth. Sydney blinked, straining to see through the darkness. She lifted her hand and held it inches from her face. She couldn't see a thing.

The darkness felt like more than an absence of light. It felt real, something with substance and weight. It had an attitude as it tried to suffocate her, pressed on her eyes and filled her ears. It pressed down on her shoulders and chest, making it hard to breath. She felt lost and afraid and reached forward to touch Jordan's back.

"I can't see a thing, Jordan." Her voice seemed small and insignificant. She spoke louder, tried to assert her being in this black void. "How do you know which way to walk?"

"I can feel a faint draft of air on my face," Jordan replied. "Let me move to the side so I'm not blocking you." He took two steps to the left. "Can you feel it now?"

Sydney lifted her face and held her breath. At first she felt nothing, then she detected a very faint sense of air moving against her cheek. "I can barely feel it."

"I know it's faint, but I'm guessing that there is air flow between the two entrances. If I keep my face to the incoming air and follow it we should find the other entrance."

"That's brilliant, Jordan," said Sydney, her voice full of admiration. Jordan never failed to amaze her. "I feel so awkward trying to walk in the dark. I could Slow Walk, but I'm afraid of getting left behind. You and Dogma are moving much faster than I can, at least until I get used to this."

Jordan thought for a moment. "Give me a couple of those strips of bed sheet. We'll tie one around my waist and attach it to another one tied around your waist. That way we won't get separated."

Sydney did as he suggested and felt much more secure when they started off again. It didn't take long for her to work out a way to keep a light, steady pressure on the strips of sheeting. Her confidence grew and they began to move forward at a faster clip.

The smooth, hard floor of the cave made walking easy.

There were few rocks underfoot to stumble over. Every once in a while they came to a shallow, dish-shaped depression. Sydney could feel the sheet strip dip and knew that Jordan had stepped down. She slid her foot forward until she felt the edge, then followed Jordan down, across, and up the opposite side.

After what seemed an eternity, she sensed the cavern walls drawing closer, but when she reached out to touch them she felt only empty space. She found the experience disorienting and a little unnerving.

They walked for what felt to Sydney like an entire day, but she knew it had only been a few hours. Her intense focus on each step she took robbed her of all sense of time. This is what it means to live in the now, she realized. Nothing else existed at that moment except for each step forward.

Caught up in her musings, Sydney didn't realize that Jordan had stopped until she walked into his solid back. "Oomph. Sorry. What's wrong?" she asked.

"The air flow is growing stronger. Can you feel it?" He took a step forward, then stopped again. "The cave floor slants down here. Watch your step."

They slowly slid their feet along the steeply angled floor, feeling their way so as not to stumble and lose their footing. The smooth floor became rippled with small peaks like waves frozen in mud which eased their descent while increasing the likelihood of a turned ankle.

There was no telling what lay at the bottom of the decline and neither of them wanted to fall into a deep, dark, chasm. The thought of being lost forever in the bowels of the earth made Sydney shudder. All through man's history civilizations had located their hells deep beneath the planet's surface and populated their caves with evil spirits. Monsters of scary proportions lay in wait in the dark.

"Stop it," she muttered to herself. "Get a grip. There are no monsters."

"I can feel the air flow now, it's definitely stronger," she said in a louder voice.

Sydney blinked and peered into the darkness. "Jordan, I think it's a little lighter up ahead. She surged forward, anxious to reach a place where she could see again.

Jordan grabbed her arm as she went to pass him. "Not so fast. We have no idea what's waiting for us at this other entrance. I vote we continue with me and Dogma in the lead. Vote carried." He gave her no chance to argue. "You keep behind me where it's safe."

Sydney grumbled but fell into place behind Jordan. Secretly she felt pleased that he wanted to protect her. The fact that he felt comfortable enough to take a leadership role lifted her spirits. She had carried a heavy guilt when she first took him away from all that he knew even though he would've died of starvation if she left him behind.

Fortunately Jordan's good nature and his love for new experiences had overcome any drawbacks from his handicap. Once freed of the familiarity of his childhood home, he had developed a spatial sixth sense that often made her forget that he was blind.

He also turned out to be an excellent traveling companion: interesting and easy-going, as well as intelligent and funny.

She found Jordan incredibly masculine and handsome and she was attracted to him in a way she had never been attracted to any male since Jake Mayo in the fifth grade. That young girl crush had lasted all the school year, until Jake had taunted her for being a lowly sheep farmer's granddaughter.

Thinking about Jordan took her mind off walking in the dark. He had kissed her three times now. The first, a gentle kiss that took place when he had explored her face with his fingers in an effort to learn what she looked like.

The second one had been a very passionate kiss after they had survived a life-threatening situation. The third kiss took place when he had surprised her on the road outside of Driftwood, South Dakota and asked to continue with her on her search for Smokey.

Since then, nothing. Sydney sighed. She still tingled when she thought about those kisses.

She lifted her head and was startled to see the faint outline of Jordan's bulk in front of her. The light was definitely growing stronger. They were closing in on the second entrance. She stepped faster and moved up to walk beside Jordan.

"Jordan, I'm sure it's getting lighter. I can make out your shape now."

Sydney sought for and found his hand. She squeezed and he squeezed back, careful not to hurt her. She laced her fingers through his, happy for the human contact.

The cave walls receded and they soon found themselves in another immense underground chamber. Light poured in from a large hole in the chamber's roof far above their heads.

"Wow. I've explored quite a few caves with my father, but I've never seen anything like this," said Sydney. "It looks as if the cave ceiling collapsed, Jordan. There's a small mountain of rock and dirt rising from the cave floor with trees and plants growing on it. The roof must be at least one hundred feet over our heads and even with the light I can't see any cave walls. This cavern must be immense."

"Can we climb out?" asked Jordan. The ground began to rise under his feet. He felt the warmth of the sun on his face and smelled the greenery growing on the hillside.

"No. The tree tops don't reach the edge of the hole. The

plants look quite lush, they must get plenty of moisture. I'm going to let Ginny and Harriet out to scratch for bugs and green shoots while I explore. I wish my father was here, he'd love this."

Sydney took off her pack and released the hens onto the hill's bottom edge. They clucked with pleasure and darted around her feet, wasting no time scratching for insects.

Sydney scrambled carefully up the side of the mountain, taking care not to trample the delicate plants. The cave-in had created a specialized biome, one able to grow more than one hundred feet below the earth's surface because of the sun's reach.

Before the upheaval this would have been a monumental discovery, written up in nature and science journals by a variety of experts. Now there was no one left to care. The thought brought her a pang of sadness. When all one's energies had to go toward surviving there was nothing left over to appreciate the natural wonders of Earth.

She found a rock to sit on near the mountain's peak and gratefully lifted her face to the sun's rays. Although she had enjoyed exploring caves with her biologist father, she had always felt a sense of relief when they climbed above ground again.

She estimated the hole overhead to be at least one hundred fifty feet across. She couldn't see above the rim and no tree branch grew close enough to touch the edge. She found a small rock and tried tossing it out of the hole but failed; the edge of the hole was too far away.

How ironic is this? she wondered. Here she stood, within twenty feet of the surface, with no way out. They would have to continue on under ground. The thought depressed her.

Sydney took her attention off the rim and looked for Jordan. She spied him circling the hill's base with Dogma at his heels. He had removed his pack and was using the iron-wood staff to poke around the large pile of dirt and rock.

Jordan sensed her gaze upon him and looked up. "Find anything to eat up there?" he called to her.

"Not yet. I'm hoping some of these greens are edible."

Jordan disappeared around the far side of the hill. A few moments later Sydney heard him shout. "Syd, you'd better come down here."

Sydney leaped to her feet and picked her way carefully around the mountain peak. When she reached the far side she stopped in wonder and amazement. Below her stretched a series of terraced gardens, all holding some type of vegetable or fruit. She identified squash, a short-eared corn, lettuce, carrot tops, amaranth, beans, raspberries, and more.

"Jordan, there's a lovely garden up here! I can't believe it. I wonder where the people are who planted this?" She descended alongside the terraces, keeping to a narrow manmade trail. She spotted Jordan as she reached the bottom and hurried over to him.

"Maybe the people who left the footprints planted the vegetables. You wouldn't believe how beautiful they look. They're terraced just like the mountain people in the Andes and China do. I'm really impressed. I bet they have to haul water from the pool we fou—" She stopped talking, mouth agape.

Seated cross-legged in the entrance of a small cave dug into the side of the hill was a slender, bald man dressed in a short ragged robe. His feet were bare and gnarly, his knees knobby and gray with ground-in dirt.

Sydney's eyes widened with surprise. The man's dark brown, leathery skin was stretched over his skull, his cheeks hollow shadows under prominent cheekbones. His bushy eyebrows and long beard were a silver gray that reminded

Sydney of her mother's pewter collection. The old man's calm, brown eyes observed them. He seemed unsurprised by their presence.

"Hi. I'm Sydney Waters and this is my friend Jordan James. We got trapped in the desert and are looking for a way back to the high ground. Can you help us?"

"What you seek is not possible. Nothing escapes the underground." The old man's voice sounded rusty and hoarse from disuse.

"Surely there must be a way to get back onto the high plateau," insisted Sydney. "We can't survive in the desert without food and water and we can't stay down in this cave forever." A chill went through Sydney's body at the thought of spending the remainder of her life wandering underground.

"What is your name?" asked Jordan.

The old man'e eyes shifted to him. "I am the Keeper. There are seven of us. We tend the light holes." His gaze shifted to Dogma. "Who is the great beast?"

Jordan adopted the man's clipped manner of speech. "She is called Dogma. She protects us."

The Keeper studied Jordan for a moment. "You are blind. Above, below, they are no different for you. You will do fine."

"What do you mean, Jordan will do fine?" Sydney was growing agitated. She didn't care for this unhelpful Keeper fellow. The fear that she might be stuck between desert and caves made her feel nervous and angry.

"We both need to get out of this cavern. Humans need sunlight you know, for vitamin D, or we get sick. People are not meant to live as moles."

"There is no way back to the surface," the Keeper repeated. "There are seven light holes. And there is Graceville."

Sydney's brow furrowed. "Do you mean Graceland? Graceland is in Tennessee, not Nebraska."

Jordan shifted beside her and gave her a light touch on her arm, willing her not to succumb to panic. "Keeper, does each light hole have a fine mountain such as yours? And do the other Keepers also have such fine gardens?"

A look of surprise crossed the Keeper's face. "How is it a blind man can see my mountain and gardens?"

"It's hard to explain, Keeper. I cannot see them with my eyes, of course, I use another sense. I can feel the size and shape of your mountain, and my friend told me of your beautiful gardens. I see you as a rainbow of light, mostly greens and blues with a little yellow. The trees and plants glow with a greenish-yellow light."

The Keeper sat in silence for a long minute. "I have heard of such a skill belonging to medicine men and gifted saints."

Sydney looked at Jordan wide-eyed. "Why didn't you tell me you can see light?" she whispered. "You're seeing auras, right? I thought only certain people with a highly developed sense of intuition or ESP could do that."

Jordan shrugged. "I don't know about the intuition part. It's a little weird, to be honest. It's a different light, more like energy, like I would expect electricity to look if I could see it. I started seeing it after my fall off the cliff. I didn't want to mention it until I knew it wasn't a side effect of the head injury."

He turned back to the Keeper. "You said there are seven light holes and each one has a Keeper. What is Graceville?"

Keeper looked past Jordan's shoulder into the distance. "Graceville sits on the edge of the Great Lake."

Jordan frowned. "Is Graceville a town? Are you saying there is an underground town near here?"

The Keeper didn't answer. He stood in one fluid motion

and disappeared inside his cave. Sydney and Jordan stared after him, unsure of how to react. Should they follow him? A short while later the Keeper popped back out with two lettuce leaves wrapped around a paste-like substance.

"Take these. It is all I have to share at the moment." He pointed off to his left. "The next light hole is a half-day's walk in that direction. There is a spring there where you can fill your water containers." He pulled his short robe tight around his bottom and lowered himself cross-legged in the mouth of his cave.

Sydney sampled her lettuce-wrap. The filling tasted of beans and ground corn. She ate half of it and gave the remainder to Dogma.

"Which way to Graceville?" she asked, licking her fingers. The wrap had made a pleasant change from eggs and jerky. She could eat a half dozen of them.

The Keeper nodded over his shoulder. "That way lies madness," he said.

3

"THAT WAY LIES MADNESS? Do you think the keeper might be a little mad himself, living underground, watching over a light hole?"

Sydney and Jordan were tied together again, even though they still walked in the fading light from the light hole. She looked at Jordan and waited for him to make a joke about the keeper, but he remained silent.

"Jordan? What do you think he meant by 'that way lies madness'?" pressed Sydney.

Jordan gave his head a slight shake and kept walking. The keeper's words bothered him more than he cared to admit. He would lay odds that there was something very wrong with the town of Graceville and he wished they didn't have to go there. He had no desire to find out about the madness. Unfortunately he could come up with no alternative. They needed to find a way out of here and the light holes were not an option.

Sydney made no further attempt at conversation. She willed the light to last, but it grew feeble and finally disappeared all together. Once again they trudged side by side through the heavy darkness, each wrapped up in their private thoughts until Sydney stumbled over an object and fell to her knees.

"Oomph. That was klutzy of me." She felt around the cave floor where she had fallen, searching for whatever had tripped her. Her hands closed on a thin, flat, curved object. She felt several more nearby.

She expanded her search and touched a round stone with long, stringy moss attached to one side. A round stone with two holes and a ridge of teeth.

"Holy crap!" She jerked her hand back and scrambled to her feet. "It's a skeleton, Jordan. I tripped over a human skeleton. I found some ribs and the skull." She shuddered. What she thought was long, stringy moss was hair. "I touched it."

She slid her foot along the ground and pushed aside several more bones. "There are dead people down here," she whispered. "Maybe the keeper was right—there is no way out of here. These people were trapped like us and died down here." Her heart hammered in her chest and she fought down the panic that threatened to overwhelm her.

Jordan reached out and grasped her shaking hand. He pulled her close to his side. "We are going to find a way out, I promise you. Get a grip on yourself. You are far more resourceful than whoever that is lying there. Keep moving forward." He took a step and tugged on her hand.

Sydney took several steps and kicked another pile of bones. "Jordan, there's more than one. What if we're in the middle of a graveyard of some sort? What if we're surrounded by hundreds of dead people?" She began to shiver.

"I'm not stepping on any skeletons so I doubt very much that we're in the middle of a graveyard. Walk closer to me."

"What-what do you think happened to them?" Sydney's imagination was running rampant. She pictured hundreds of skeletons with arms outstretched as if to claw themselves toward their destination. It took a great deal of effort to force the image from her mind.

"I don't know why they died, Sydney. There doesn't seem to be anything to eat down here except for what the keepers grow under the light holes. Maybe these people starved to death. I don't think they were killed by a dangerous animal, there doesn't seem to be much of anything living in this cave."

Sydney slid around the bones and huddled closer to Jordan. She relaxed somewhat when she realized that he was right; there were no skeletons where he walked.

"I don't think we're in the cave anymore," she said thoughtfully. She felt much calmer now that she wasn't kicking people's bones around. "I think when we came down that long incline right before we met the keeper that we descended into the main body of the aquifer. The light holes must be where the top of the aquifer came close to the land surface. The thinner crust of earth collapsed when the water level dropped."

"That's a reasonable theory," answered Jordan. "If you're right, then this cavern might extend across the entire width of Nebraska. I wonder if the Great Lake the keeper mentioned is a remnant of the aquifer?"

Sydney didn't bother to answer. She concentrated on remaining positive and prayed that they would soon stumble across a way out of this endless hole in the ground.

They spent a restless night with no fire and no food and started off again as soon as they awoke. Sydney packed her sleeping bag in the never relenting darkness by feel and thought of what life must be like for Jordan, never having light to guide him.

She didn't miss light only to see what she was doing; she missed seeing colors and feeling the sun's warm rays. Just like in the Wizard of Oz movie where color brought Kansas to life, color made the world vibrant and exciting.

Jordan's world was a monotone, perpetually black. He couldn't even experience the rosy glow of sunlight behind his closed eyelids.

But that wasn't quite true anymore, she realized, as she slipped on her pack. If Jordan now saw auras, he was seeing the world in a way that most people didn't even believe possible. He was tuning into the energy of all living things.

Ginny and Harriet interrupted her thoughts. They grumbled in chicken speak as their cages rocked. Afraid they'd get lost, Sydney hadn't dared to let them loose in the pitch dark cave and the hens were unhappy about their extended confinement.

You could've found them."

"What?" asked Jordan.

Sydney hadn't realized that she had spoken aloud. "I didn't dare to let Ginny and Harriet out of their cages because I wouldn't be able to find them again in this black hole. But you would've seen their auras, right? You would've been able to find them."

"Maybe. As long as they weren't too far away, I think I could have located them, yes. The light they give off is fairly soft and it's small so they need to be nearby for me to see them."

"What do you see when you look at me?" She envied

Jordan's ability to see auras. It would be amazing to see the essence of all living things, to experience the energy fields that burned at the core of every being.

Jordan considered for a moment. "You look like a stretched oval, sort of egg-shaped, and your light is a bright, warm yellow-white." He didn't tell her that there was a strange dent in her aura, as if some part of her had gone missing.

"That's different from the way you saw the keeper, isn't it?" They finished tying themselves together and started walking. Sydney had no clue how Jordan kept track of the direction they walked. If it was left up to her they'd be traveling in circles. Somehow though, she knew Jordan was keeping them on course.

"That's right. I hadn't really thought about it. With the keeper I saw more of a colored rainbow radiating around his head and torso. With you I see your whole body as a whitish egg. Since you're the only two people I've encountered since I developed my new sense I have no idea why I see you differently."

Hours passed with only the sound of their booted steps to break up the silence. Just as Sydney thought she might be going mad from the unrelenting darkness, Jordan gripped her arm and held her still.

"What is it?" she hissed, every cell alert and straining.

"Shush. I thought I heard something." Jordan slowly turned his head back and forth and listened, but he heard nothing more.

"It must have been an auditory hallucination," he said. He caught a faint glow moving toward them.

"Don't move," he whispered. "There's someone or something out there, headed toward us. Stand very still and don't make a sound."

Jordan watched the glow grow closer. The light separated into bands of color. A human aura, he realized, but with dark and murky colors; they weren't clear the way he saw the keeper's colors.

He felt Dogma tense against his leg and knew she had spotted whoever approached. He relaxed a little. The aura wasn't a hallucination, something Jordan had feared when he first saw the light approaching.

"Jordan? Is someone out there?" Sydney whispered. Her eyes felt dry from staring into the darkness as she strained to see something, anything besides black.

Jordan squeezed her hand, willing her to be quiet, but it was too late. The aura changed direction and headed straight for them. He wondered if it's owner could see in the dark.

The aura stopped a short distance away. Dogma growled softly and the aura retreated several steps. "Who goes there?" demanded a thin, reedy voice.

"Jordan James." Jordan saw no reason to mention Sydney until he could be sure the aura posed no threat. "Who are you?" he asked. He watched the aura's bands of light shifting but they never cleared. His intuition told him that this was not a healthy aura, this person was ill in some way he couldn't yet see.

"I am one of the king's court. Sir William of the order of the green knights of Graceville. You will come with me now or I will be obliged to kill you. That is the law of the land. All trespassers are required to have an audience with the King."

"Where is Graceville? I don't see any light ahead." Jordan kept his voice light and friendly even though the aura's claim of knighthood and mention of a king worried him. Given the skeletons Sydney had stumbled upon, he had no doubt that the threat of death was real.

"We are not far from the Great Lake and the Kingdom of

Graceville. You have entered into the forbidden zone." The knight's voice climbed. "All trespassers are required to be brought before the King. You will follow me now or die." The aura started moving away.

Jordan placed a hand on Dogma's hind end and gently pushed her to a sit. He leaned close to Sydney and whispered very softly into her ear. "Stay with Dogma. Follow us at a discreet distance, but don't let him know you are here. Take your boots off so you can't be heard. Stay hidden near the outskirts of Graceville and I will find you, I promise." He planted a quick kiss on her hair.

"I will be pleased to go with you, Sir William, to meet your king," Jordan said aloud to the retreating aura. "Does your king have a name?"

The aura fluttered a moment, then flared and receded. "He is the king. The king is the king. Make haste. The king awaits." He waited for Jordan to join him and then hastened off into the darkness.

***

Sydney removed her boots as quickly and quietly as she could. She heard Jordan talking to the knight and knew he was trying to cover any sounds she might make. She touched Dogma, releasing her from the sit command, and headed after Jordan.

She carried her boots in her hands, not wanting to take the time to stash them in her pack. The aquifer floor felt cold and rough on her bare feet. The dank odor of earth never touched by the sun filled her nostrils. Funny how she hadn't noticed that while Jordan was at her side.

She prayed she wouldn't step in any slimy grossness, or stumble across any more dead bodies. The last thought made her shudder in revulsion. She was not enjoying this under-ground adventure at all. The darkness grew solid and filled her lungs, making it hard to breath.

She would go mad if she didn't get back to the surface soon.

She followed the sound of the two men as fast as she could, afraid that if she lost them she would be left to wander alone in the dark cavern until she died.

4

JORDAN KEPT up a running patter to give Sydney something to follow. He worried that by taking her to Graceville he was leading her into danger, but he knew that she would panic if she were left to wander the dark aquifer on her own. At least he would know that she was nearby. After his audience with the king he would retrace his steps and find her.

"Who is the king?" he asked Sir William, hoping to glean more information about their destination.

"Are you stupid? The king is the king, of course." Sir William's voice sounded taut with anger. "Every kingdom must have a king. Every king must have his knights to protect and defend the kingdom. I am a green knight." The words were said with a great deal of pride.

"Who made the king king?"

Sir William stopped walking. Obviously the question befuddled him. After a moment he started walking again. "The king declared himself king," he stated firmly. "That is all there is to it. You will see. No more questions. The king will tell you what he wants you to know."

They walked in silence for several minutes. Jordan

listened for Sydney's steps but heard nothing. He became concerned that without his voice to follow she might lose them. He had to make noise somehow, but Sir William had forbidden him to ask any more questions. Inspiration struck. He began to sing softly.

Sir William did not tell him to keep quiet. When Jordan finished the song he requested another.

"The king's court does not possess a minstrel," he said, after Jordan finished singing a third song. "I will be rewarded for finding you and bringing you to the king. He will be very pleased."

Sir William sounded very pleased with himself. He chuckled, a high-pitched eerie sound. "I will be rewarded," he repeated several times.

"How much farther to the kingdom?" asked Jordan in a loud voice after several minutes of silence. He prayed they didn't have much farther to go. He knew that Sydney had to be struggling to keep up with them without making noise.

He risked a look over his shoulder. Relief washed over him when he saw her egg-shaped light. Dogma's squat light pressed against Sydney's side. Jordan frowned in concern; she had fallen too far behind. If she didn't move faster she would lose them.

He caught a brief glimpse of the chicken's faint glow bouncing near the area of Sydney's shoulders. He prayed they wouldn't squawk and give away Sydney's presence.

"We are almost there, minstrel. Put your hands out, you will soon feel the rampart."

"A rampart? You built a stone wall surrounding the kingdom?" He couldn't keep the disbelief from his voice. Perhaps the keeper was right, this way lay madness. Sir William certainly sounded a little whacked, and even with his limited experience with auras, Jordan knew that the knight's was an unhealthy blend of off-colors.

"We have no stone, fool," replied Sir William scornfully. "Are you stupid? Our rampart is made of wood. Everyone knows that a kingdom is protected by moats and ramparts. The Great Lake protects the kingdom of Graceville on one side and the rampart keeps the enemy from surprising us on the other."

Jordan wondered about the king's enemies. He stretched out both arms. He sensed the ceiling slanting closer overhead. Within several steps his fingers touched a rough wood board. Sir William turned to the left and walked along the rampart wall. Jordan dragged his hand lightly along the wall as he followed the knight.

"Where did you get the wood for the wall?"

"It was a gift from the Old World. The light hole expanded and brought us the wood to expand our kingdom. The King declared it a sign that we were meant to establish the new Graceville here beside the lake."

They reached the end of the wall. Sir William stopped abruptly. "Now you will see how clever the king is. We descend here."

Jordan felt a moment of panic. He could see nothing, but he sensed a great void below him. The scent of water tinged with the faint smell of wood smoke filled the air.

"The steps are steep. Go slow. If you fall to your death the king will not be pleased."

"The king isn't the only one who won't be pleased if I fall to my death," muttered Jordan.

"What did you say?" asked Sir William. His voice took on a panicked edge. "No, no. Are you stupid? What are you doing? You must step here."

Jordan didn't want to let the knight know that he was

blind. He couldn't say why, but it seemed important to keep his affliction a secret. He wondered how he could cover his inability to see and was struck with an inspiration. Sir William had mentioned a light hole; he hoped that meant there was light over the town.

"I can't see." He forced a little whine into his voice. "I've been wandering in the dark for so long that the light has temporarily blinded me. You'll have to guide my descent or I will surely fall. The king will not be pleased if you allow his new minstrel to perish before he gets to hear me perform."

He watched Sir William's aura flash. A dull red swirled through the darker colors. He's agitated, thought Jordan. He didn't know how he knew that, but he felt sure that the red in the knight's aura meant anger and frustration. The red suddenly winked out.

"Give me your hand and I will guide you. I will not allow you to fall and deprive me of my reward." Sir William took Jordan's hand and slowly guided him down the steps. The knight let out an audible sigh when they reached the bottom safely. He dropped Jordan's hand. "Come. It is time to meet the king."

Jordan tried not to stumble as Sir William hastened him along. The green knight seemed to grow more agitated with every step. His aura flashed and spiked and his voice grew higher and tighter.

"Must see the king. You're too slow. We have to get to the king. It's late, it's late. We must see the king. You're too slow."

Jordan didn't dare interrupt Sir William's tirade. He kept a careful distance from the strange aura and walked as quickly as could. He wished he could see the town. He smelled water and sensed they were close to the lake, but he had no concept of the buildings that comprised the town or the layout. Finding Sydney was going to be more difficult than he had realized.

Sir William stopped abruptly, causing Jordan to stumble and lose his balance as he tried to avoid plowing into the knight. He put his hand out and caught Sir William on the arm. Sir William squawked and pulled away.

"We're here. We're here. Be quick. Be quick. The king is waiting." Sir William scurried ahead.

<hr>

Sydney lost track of Jordan and his captor several times, but she knew Dogma would always know her master's location so she didn't panic. She kept her fingers wrapped in Dogma's ruff so she wouldn't lose track of the great beast and strained to hear the men they followed.

Her feet grew numb from walking on the cold rough stone. She longed to put her stockings and boots back on, but couldn't risk the time it would take, nor the chance that Jordan's captor would hear her booted footsteps.

They seemed to walk forever, but she knew it hadn't been all that long before she saw the dim glow of a light hole. The long, horizontal crack of light made no sense until she reached the wooden wall. The wall blocked the light except for a narrow space between the lower ceiling and the top edge of the wall.

Sydney followed the wall toward her left, careful to wait until Jordan and his captor disappeared around the end of the wall before she drew closer. She peered around the wall's end in time to see a skinny, middle-aged man dressed in green scrubs guide Jordan down a set of rough-shaped steps cut into a cliff face.

At the bottom of the cliff lay a vast body of water. It

stretched into the gloom with no sign of a distant shore. This had to be the Great Lake the keeper had mentioned, she realized.

Between the cliff and the lake stood a town that she assumed was Graceville; little more than a collection of odd wooden shanties built in a single line along the shore of the lake.

She watched Jordan and his captor enter a square, two-story building located in the center of the town. While the other buildings were all built of wood, this one, the largest in the small town, was constructed of a dark yellow brick.

Brick? How could that be? She stared at the large structure, trying to understand. Then it hit her—the building had fallen through the light hole and landed mostly intact. The first floor had collapsed into a pile of bricks, but the two stories above had survived the fall.

It must have been a grand building at one time, she mused as she inspected the decorative brick work and a widow's walk on the rooftop. A large blue and yellow flag hung from one of the building's two chimneys, but the thing that caught her eye the most and sent a chill down her spine were the windows. Tall and elegantly proportioned, they were covered with narrow, black bars.

She turned to inspect the wall at the top of the cliff. The side facing the lake was well lit by the massive light hole that stood over the town and a small part of the lake below. The wall appeared to be built of a hodgepodge of different sized boards, some with various colors of paint still visible, and it extended far beyond the limits of Graceville.

The wall also reached almost to the cavern's ceiling. That explained why it remained dark in the cavern in spite of the nearby light hole. The wall camouflaged the town and light hole from unwanted visitors.

She slid out of her backpack and sat down to put her boots on. Her feet welcomed the warmth of her wool socks and boots and Sydney's spirits rose. She leaned against the wall and contemplated the scene below. She would have to wait until dusk before she dared to descend the cliff steps and search for Jordan.

After several hours wait Sydney grew restless and decided to explore the opposite end of the wall. She covered the hen's cages to keep them quiet and left them with her pack. She took Dogma with her.

Afraid that she might be seen from below, she walked along the dark side of the wall, trailing her hand along the rough boards so she wouldn't lose her way, until she reached the far end.

Sydney stepped out from behind the far end of the wall and regarded the the town from this new perspective. The Great Lake still disappeared into the gloom. She saw nothing but the town of Graceville on its shore. The remaining shoreline was barren.

No boats plied the lake's surface. She wondered if fish lived in the lake. It seemed doubtful, given that the lake was a remnant of the huge aquifer that once filled the cavern.

She stood and watched the town for several minutes, but saw little activity. The occasional person appeared from one of the shanties and scurried into the large brick building. There was no action around the lake shore and no one walked the only street. From what she could see, Graceville was a very sleepy town.

She turned to make her way back along the wall and was struck in the face with a wiggling, snakelike object. A small scream escaped her lips and she leaped backward. Dogma woofed and growled at her side.

"Hold the end of the ladder, for Pete's sake. Are you stupid?" The voice came from over Sydney's head.

She looked up and saw a round light in the aquifer ceiling. The outline of a person's torso blocked part of the hole. She grabbed the thick, snakelike object and discovered that it was actually a rope ladder similar to the fire escape ladder her mother had once stowed in her second-floor bedroom closet.

She felt someone climbing down and automatically tightened her grip on the ladder. She tried to see the speaker, but small bits of earth fell into her face, forcing her to look down to avoid getting any in her eyes.

Too late, it occurred to her that she did not want to be discovered hanging around Graceville. She debated running but the person was almost to the bottom of the ladder; if she tried to run now she would surely be captured. She decided to brazen it out.

The ladder climber reached the bottom and leaped the last few feet to the ground, clanking when he landed. She saw a small middle-aged man with an almost non-existent hairline and a round belly.

He turned and looked straight at Sydney. Everything about his face looked pinched and sharp. His long blade of a nose, small thin mouth, pointed chin, and tiny dark eyes that darted back and forth reminded Sydney of a ferret.

Dressed in dingy blue scrubs, Ferret Face carried a stained florescent orange sack on his belt. The bag was the source of the clanking, she now realized.

"Much obliged. No peanut butter, but a good haul today. The king will be pleased." He bowed to Sydney and scurried off toward the cliff steps.

Sydney stared after him. The man had exhibited no interest in her whatsoever. All he seemed to care about was getting his haul, whatever that was, to the king. She wondered who the king could be and what the strange man found to scavenge in the desert overhead.

Overhead. Ferret Face had just descended from the surface. A thrill of excitement shot through her. She had discovered a way to return to the surface. Once she found Jordan they could escape this vast natural dungeon.

She started up the ladder after commanding Dogma to stay. Her arms began to tremble with fatigue before she reached the top. Climbing a rope ladder was not an easy task, especially when she was weak from lack of food.

She reached the edge of the hole and peered out. The opposite end of the rope ladder was fastened to a large tree stump. She climbed another rung and rested her arms on the hole's rim and looked about.

She was on the edge of a small town, a real town, not like the one below. A great wall of tumbleweed stood piled against the side of the nearest house. The house appeared to be empty.

Sydney squeezed the rest of the way out of the hole and crouched beside it as she searched for signs of danger.

She hadn't forgotten about the Desperate Ones. They could be anywhere. She shuddered at the memory of the evil men who had killed her sister and grandfather and driven her from her home.

The ordeal of traveling through the aquifer had buried the memory of losing Shannon, but here on the surface the pain and fear and self-loathing all came flooding back. She needed to be very careful. She had only her knife and Dogma waited below. She wished the giant beast was at her side.

Sydney waited for several long minutes but nothing stirred. The town appeared to be abandoned. She stood slowly and walked toward the nearest house. She circled around to the front and found the entry door hanging open. Sand covered the narrow porch and the hall floor inside.

"Is anyone home?" she called softly. She heard no reply. She searched the house and found nothing of interest inside. The only items that remained were large and heavy pieces of furniture: bed frames, a sofa and chairs, a china cabinet with smashed glass doors. Whatever had been displayed inside the cabinet was gone.

She thought about the clanging sack and realized Ferret Face had most likely searched the town for items to salvage. She left the house and walked deeper into the town, noting the modest homes that lined the streets.

This had been an average, prospering town, she realized. One of the many farm-based small communities that dotted the plains states and managed to survive on a limited economic base. Several of the houses were partly demolished, their interiors left exposed to the ravages of the weather.

The storefronts on Main Street boasted broken windows guarded by the skeletons of dead trees that once graced the central street through town. Tumbleweed rolled and gathered everywhere she looked, locking together until some of the impenetrable masses reached to the building roof peaks.

She wondered why the town had been abandoned. Since The Upheaval the chances of survival were higher in a small farming community than in the larger cities. The people who once lived here must have known that. Why did they leave?

It didn't take long to find the light hole. Below, the hole in the ground brought light and was appropriately named; standing on the surface she could see that the light hole was actually a gigantic sinkhole.

She kept well away from the edge, afraid that it could break away and carry her to her death. The hole had taken a portion of the town with it when it collapsed into the aquifer. A few homes stood on the edge, ripped open, exposing their innards to the ravages of the wind and sand.

Perhaps the sinkhole forced the citizens to abandon their town. She hoped they had found another community willing to take them in.

Sydney turned away from the hole and headed back down Main Street. She came upon a building made from the same dark yellow bricks as the one she'd seen below in the center of Graceville. Unlike the rest of the stores and diners on Main Street, the building's windows stood intact.

Curious, she walked up the wide cement steps and tried the door. It opened easily under her hand.

Sydney hesitated, then cautiously entered and closed the door behind her. The interior of the building felt pleasantly cool and was free of sand. Worn and scratched plastic chairs sat in short neat rows in front of a waist-high laminated counter. A long, wooden bench ran along each side wall.

Sydney let herself behind the counter and walked down the short hall. There were only two rooms opening off the hall. The left-hand room held a desk and chair and book-shelves filled with farm bureau bulletins, US census reports, and legal material for the state of Nebraska. She closed the office door and walked across the hall.

The second room held metal file cabinets and boxes of copier paper and unused file folders. Stacked along one wall were taped cardboard boxes stamped "Feminine Hygiene." A small pile of emptied cartons lay neatly stacked against a file cabinet.

Curious, Sydney pulled a full box off a stack and set it on the floor. She pulled her knife and slit the carton open. The box contained a dozen large, unbranded cans of peanut butter. Apparently the scavenger had not searched this building yet. She tried several other boxes and found luncheon meat and freeze-dried military rations.

A bonanza! Food in the underground had been practically non-existent. They were slowly starving while they tried to find their way back to the surface. Sydney had felt Dogma's ribs the last time she had petted her. The keeper's generous but small meal had been too little to help alleviate the gnawing pain of hunger.

Sydney made her way out of the municipal building back to the stores where she eventually found a sack large enough to carry some of the food she had found. She concentrated on the items that would give them the most calories and not weigh too much. Much as she hated to pass them up, the peanut butter cans were too large and heavy to carry.

She packed as many freeze-dried meals as she could carry and included half a dozen cans of luncheon meat and several meat stews for Dogma. She hefted the sack, decided to add a few more freeze-dried meals, and made her way back to the front of the building. On her way out she stopped to read the notices tacked to three large bulletin boards, the most recent one several years old now.

The red-lettered notice warned the town's residents to check and stock their emergency kits with water and batteries, citing the increased frequency of earthquakes and tornadoes in the area. Sydney shook her head and moved to the next cork board. In normal times those emergency kits would have saved lives. They were woefully inadequate against The Upheaval.

Twenty minutes later Sydney closed the door of the town office behind her. Her hand trembled slightly. She hurried back to the house half-buried in tumbleweed and looked for the stump with the rope ladder. Once she found it she wasted no time descending back into the aquifer.

The approaching twilight made the trip back along the wall more difficult, but Sydney didn't slacken her pace. She needed to find Jordan and get him out of Graceville as soon as possible. She thought about what she had learned on the surface and broke into a slow jog.

The brick building with barred windows that sat in the center of Graceville was a mental hospital. It housed those too incompetent to care for themselves as well as the criminally insane. It was the latter that made her tremble.

Graceville was a town populated by lunatics, some of whom were dangerous killers. The keeper was being literal when he had said this way lay madness. And now Jordan was in the middle of it.

5

JORDAN TOOK a step after Sir William and immediately tripped and fell over a pile of hard objects. He went down on his hands and knees and grunted when a sharp corner bit into his shin. He ran his fingers over the objects and found he had fallen on a pile of bricks. Bricks that had rough mortar clinging to them, so they were from a demolished building.

"Hang on a minute, Sir William. I may need a guide through this." Jordan carefully got to his feet and slid a foot forward. He felt more bricks. He slid his foot to the side, looking for the path through the brick pile.

"Are you stupid? Follow me, the king awaits." Sir William impatiently grabbed at Jordan's free hand and tugged him forward.

Jordan stumbled again and barely managed to stay upright. He felt like a young child being dragged along by an impatient parent. He didn't care for Sir William calling him stupid, but he had to admit that he must look that way to the strange man.

He grimly tightened his grip on Sir William and stayed

with the knight in spite of the obstacles underfoot. Several times he stubbed his toes and bit back a curse. Fortunately they soon entered a building and the footing once again became smooth and uniform.

Their footsteps echoed inside the building. Jordan realized they were walking down a long hallway. He saw no other auras in the vicinity and some of his tension eased.

Sir William dropped Jordan's hand. His aura began to rise above Jordan's head. It took Jordan a moment to realize the knight was ascending stairs. They climbed eight steps, hit a landing and turned left, then climbed ten more steps and went through a heavy metal door.

Jordan's senses told him they were in another hallway. He heard voices up ahead and saw three auras bunched together. They all exhibited the same murky off-colors as Sir William's aura.

The off-colored auras worried Jordan. Something was wrong with these auras, although he had no idea what. Seeing auras was too new an experience and he simply didn't know enough about them to determine why these bothered him so.

Jordan wondered why Sydney's aura, other than the dark hole, shone so clear and bright compared to the ones he was observing. The keeper's aura had also been sharp and clear. He watched the three auras closely as they approached, but no one moved.

Sir William propelled him through a doorway into a room. The room held many auras, all moving about in a herky-jerky motion that made him feel a little dizzy. They all displayed the same muddy colors as Sir William.

The green knight grabbed Jordan's arm again and marched him to an aura that sat motionless in the center of the gyrating group. Sir William dropped Jordan's arm and his aura bent downward. Was he bowing? wondered Jordan.

"Your majesty, I have brought you a wandering minstrel for your pleasure,"

"Who Are You?" The voice sounded deep, smooth, and honeyed, like a lovely bass oboe. It charmed Jordan and made him smile.

"I am-." Jordan caught himself. Perhaps it would be best if he had a title also. He couldn't be sure, but he suspected he was facing a strange cult whose members all played some fantasy role. "I am Sir Jordan James the Piano Man," he finished smoothly. "And whom do I have the honor of meeting?"

The voice's aura flashed acid blues and greens. "Who Am I? King of the Whole Wide World."

So this was the king. Jordan waited, unsure what to do or say next. He wished he had Sydney with him. He had never been very good at make-believe. He had preferred sports to video games and played baseball until the accident that left him blind. After that all his creativity had been channeled into his music career.

"Stand By Me," the pleasant voice ordered.

Jordan took two steps closer. How close did the king want him to stand? he wondered.

"Stop Where You Are."

Jordan felt something grab his staff. He automatically tried to pull it away, but he was no match for the king's strength. He heard several "oohs" and "ahs" from the others in the room. The auras stopped bouncing and leaned closer.

"That's All Right," said the king.

"What's all right, your majesty? My staff? It was a gift from a very good friend. I would hate to lose it. She carved it for her grandfather who is now deceased and then gifted it to me." Jordan had a feeling the king wasn't listening to him. He heard the onlookers whispering behind him.

"Look, the king has a proper scepter now."

"Ah, the king has a royal staff. It's good. Sir Jordan the Piano Man has brought the king a gift."

Jordan frowned, but there was nothing he could do about his staff at the moment. The king started to sing softly. It took Jordan a moment to recognize Love Me Tender by Elvis Presley. He heard other voices join in, mostly out of tune and worse, out of sync.

He tried not to wince as the ensuing noise grated on his ears. Fortunately it did not go on for very long.

The king stopped singing abruptly. "Stranger In the Crowd," he said. "Talk About the Good Times."

Talk about the good times? Was the king asking him to talk about himself? The room became silent. Jordan could feel them waiting. He took a deep breath and let it out.

"Ah, well, let's see. I traveled here from central Iowa. I've performed musical concerts all over the world. I've played for the German Chancellor and the Queen of England and the aborigines of Australia."

At the mention of the queen the group broke out in wild applause.

"Sir Jordan played for our queen!"

"That's Someone You Never Forget," said the king. "What A Wonderful Life. Ready Teddy? Shake, Rattle, and Roll."

"You want me to sing?" Jordan was having a hard time following the king's strange way of talking.

"Sing! Sing!" echoed the king's court. They began to clap and chant. "Sing! Sing!"

Jordan thought for a moment. He wished he had a piano to accompany him, he had never tried to perform rock and roll with only his voice. He thought of the king singing Love Me Tender and guessed his majesty was an Elvis fan.

Jordan launched into an old favorite of his sister's, an Elvis Presley classic titled "A Little Less Conversation, A Little More Action."

The king joined him and the auras in the room once again began to bounce up and down and whirl around, often careening off one another.

What a nuthouse, thought Jordan as he and the king finished the song to wild applause. I wonder what happens next?

He didn't have long to wait for the answer. A new aura entered the room, the colors off in a way he was beginning to identify with this group.

"Your majesty," said the new aura, coming to a stop beside Jordan. "I have returned. I regret to inform you there is no peanut butter to be found anywhere." A collective groan escaped from the king's court.

Apparently peanut butter is a favorite treat in Graceville, thought Jordan. Come to think of it, he was rather fond of peanut butter himself. He couldn't remember how long it had been since he had enjoyed a good peanut butter and bacon sandwich.

The thought of peanut butter reminded him of his hunger. His stomach growled loudly and he wondered if these people were going to feed him.

"You're a Heartbreaker," said the king. "I'm All Shook Up."

"I'm sorry, your majesty, I looked in every kitchen. I did find these."

Jordan heard a clink and the court oohed. He wondered what they found so interesting. He took a step back. What if the newcomer had pulled a weapon on the king? But no. The court didn't sound frightened. He allowed himself to relax a bit.

"Finders Keepers, Losers Weepers," said the king.

"I could use those, Sir Henry of the Blue Order." A woman's voice. Several other woman cried, "Me too! Me too!"

Jordan turned toward the first speaker and inspected her aura. Unfortunately he could detect no difference between her aura and the men's in the room. So much for being able to tell male from female unless they spoke. At least he could "see" the people, he consoled himself, albeit in an odd fashion.

"Hands Off! Hard Headed Woman." The king sounded angry. His voice rumbled deep in his chest. "For the Millionth and Last Time. Get Back."

"But your majesty," whined the woman, "what will you do with jars of makeup and lipstick? These are women's things."

The room fell silent. Jordan found himself holding his breath with the others while he waited for the king's response.

"Girls! Girls! Girls! I'll Never Stand in Your Way."

Apparently the king had changed his mind.

Several auras rushed forward with eager cries and fell upon the hapless Sir Henry. Within moments they retreated to a corner with their prizes. The volume rose in the room as everyone began to talk and argue.

"Your majesty, would you like me to show Sir Jordan to his room?" A new voice at Jordan's shoulder broke through the cacophony.

Jordan turned and inspected the speaker's aura. He felt relieved to see that it burned slightly clearer than the other auras in the room. It wasn't clear and bright like Sydney's, but its colors were definitely less murky than those of the king's court. Jordan turned back to the king, suddenly anxious to get away from this odd group of people.

"Don't Think Twice, It's Alright."

"Follow me." The voice gripped Jordan's elbow and led him from the room.

"You're blind, aren't you?" asked the voice as they made their way down the staircase.

"How did you know? I thought I hid it fairly well," answered Jordan. He reached out to feel the wall and found the stair railing. He missed his staff and wondered if he'd ever get it back from the king.

"I recognized your name. I was listening from the hallway. How on earth did you end up in Graceville?" The voice stopped and Jordan heard a door open. "Watch your step along here. There's a lot of debris from when the sinkhole opened and the hospital dropped in."

Jordan stopped. "Hospital? A hospital fell into a sinkhole and landed intact?" A crazy image of a large hospital teetering on the edge of a hole and sliding out of sight sprung into his mind. How he wished he could see this place!

His companion chuckled. "Not entirely intact. We lost the first floor. It was crushed when the hospital landed, hence the debris around the building. No great loss, though. The first floor held the staff offices and visitor's room."

He grabbed Jordan's hand. "Let me guide you through here so you don't fall and hurt yourself. An untended wound can be a death sentence down here." He guided Jordan to Graceville's only street and then dropped his hand.

"Who were all those people with the king?" asked Jordan. "And who is the king? His manner of speech seemed odd to me, like he was speaking in riddles, only they weren't riddles, they mostly made sense."

"You didn't recognize him? His majesty is Elvis Presley, of

course. Everyone knows that Elvis is the king. His speech may have sounded strange to you because he only speaks in song titles. It's amazing when you think about it. He remembers all four hundred song titles that he ever recorded. We're very fortunate that he still has his wonderful voice and remembers most of the lyrics to his biggest hits."

Jordan was struck dumb. Did his companion actually believe Elvis Presley was living in Graceville? Apparently so. Any man who believed he was Elvis Presley was surely a nutcase. Which made his followers kooks as well.

He wondered why he didn't feel more worried about the situation than he did. Perhaps it was because he never felt threatened by the king, Jordan decided. The man who believed he was Elvis seemed harmless.

"Why didn't the king name this town Graceland?"

"The king didn't name this town. There's a town on the surface called Farmington. The hospital was the main employer in Farmington before the world fell apart. The orderlies and nurses dubbed the hospital Graceville when the king came to live there. They didn't want to be confused with the other Graceland you see."

He stopped and opened a door. "Here we are. Home sweet home. Please come in and join me for my evening meal." He ushered Jordan inside and guided him to a hard chair.

"I apologize for the lack of comfortable furniture. We have to make do with what we can scrounge or what falls down the light hole. The same goes for food. We're fortunate to have the lake nearby and a very large light hole so we can grow enough to sustain us."

Jordan listened as his companion rustled about the room. He sensed that the room was small and mostly bare. "Thank you for sharing with me, I deeply appreciate it, but you have me at a disadvantage, sir. You know my name, but I don't know yours."

"I am Sir Thomas of the white order." The aura sketched a quick bow.

Jordan heard the crackle of flames. "Where do you get the fuel for a fire, Sir Thomas?"

"We are burning what remains of the homes in Farmington. The soup will be hot in a few minutes."

The smell of warming vegetables soon filled the room. Jordan's stomach growled in anticipation of a hot meal. A short while later Sir Thomas handed him a handled bowl of soup and he ate in silence, savoring every drop. The soup had no seasoning, but to Jordan it tasted every bit as good as a well-seasoned meal from his past.

When he'd scraped every drop from the bowl he set it on the floor beside him and stretched his legs. He clasped his hands on his happy stomach and thanked Sir Thomas for the meal. "I'm surprised that someone with a mental disorder as acute as the king's wasn't committed to a psychiatric hospital for his own good," he said without thinking.

His comment was met with several moments of silence. Jordan swallowed. Sir Thomas believed the king was Elvis. Did he think Jordan had just accused him of mental incompetence as well?

"I thought you understood, Sir Jordan. The king lived in the hospital."

For a long moment Jordan didn't comprehend Sir Thomas's statement. Then the other man's words sunk in.

"You mean the hospital that fell through the light hole was a mental hospital?" he asked, incredulous. A cold wave of shock shivered down his spine. "I thought you were referring to a hospital that treats medical problems. Broken bones, fevers, cancer, that sort of thing. You meant a mental hospital?"

Suddenly he didn't feel quite as relaxed sitting in Sir Thomas's bare room. He pulled in his legs and straightened in the hard chair, his body tensed.

"Mental asylum would be a more accurate term, Sir Jordan," answered Sir Thomas with a trace of humor in his voice.

"I assume you were a staff member at the asylum?" said Jordan hopefully.

"Absolutely not. We got rid of all the staff. I'm one of the good guys."

Jordan hid his shock with an effort. What sort of crazy world had he stumbled into? And what did Sir Thomas mean when he said they had gotten rid of the staff? He sent up a silent prayer that Sydney knew enough to stay out of sight.

It seemed the town of Graceville was as dangerous as Driftwood had been. At least in Driftwood the bad guys were all of the criminal class and therefore predictable. And they were easy to tell apart from the good guys.

He wished he had known that the keeper was being literal when he said this way lay madness. Next time someone warned him he vowed he would pay closer attention.

Jordan wondered what he should do next.

His host had already dismissed their conversation and moved on to more pressing issues. "We need to find you a bed. Tomorrow I'll ask a couple friends to help me build you a room of your own, but for tonight you'll have to sleep in the hospital. None of us has more than one sleeping spot so I have no place for an overnight guest."

Jordan cleared his throat. He would probably regret this, but he needed to know just who he was dealing with. "Ah, Sir

Thomas, do you mind telling me why you were living in the, ah, asylum?" He held his breath as he waited for Sir Thomas's reply.

"Not at all, my friend. My father sent me to Graceville when I was seventeen. He claimed it was because I had issues controlling my anger and I liked to set fire to things, but I know the truth."

Jordan wasn't sure he wanted to hear the rest of this but he felt compelled. "And what is the truth, Sir Thomas?" He kept his tone light, as if they were discussing the weather.

"He wanted to get me out of the way of course. My parents had pretended to adopt a little orphan boy, but I knew better. He really came from a wealthy family that didn't want him any longer and they paid my parents to take him in."

Jordan pressed. "I still don't understand why they had to send you to Graceville." He watched as Sir Thomas's aura flashed wildly and the colors darkened. Jordan now realized what the murky auras meant—they signified mental instability. He suppressed a shudder.

"Are you stupid?" Sir Thomas's voice took on a menacing edge. "The little boy didn't want to share my mother with me so he made up stories about me and my parents believed them. I nipped that in the bud right away, I'll tell you." Pride and satisfaction replaced the menace in his tone. Sir Thomas's aura stabilized.

"You did? How did you manage that?" Jordan was fascinated in spite of his host's dangerous personality.

"I set fire to the little prick of course. Took care of my traitorous mother too. Her love belonged to me, not some stupid asshole boy she found on the streets and felt sorry for."

Sir Thomas's harsh breathing filled the small room for

several minutes. Jordan wondered if he had pushed the other man too far. He tried to come up with a plan if his host decided to attack him, but knew there was little he could do if Sir Thomas bashed him in the head from behind.

Jordan breathed a little easier when his host's aura lightened and calmed. He decided he had heard enough of Sir Thomas's twisted thinking. It was past time to change the subject. "I think I'm ready for bed now, Sir Thomas. It's been a long day. Will you help me find a place to sleep?"

"Of course, Sir Jordan. I will escort you back to the king's castle and find you an unused room. Tomorrow you will be put to work and I will attend to constructing a shanty of your own. You will soon be one of us."

Not bloody likely, thought Jordan as Sir Thomas led him from the small room. Unless he was stranded there forever—then he just might lose his own mind and become one of the deranged.

Sydney fed Dogma one of the cans of stew she had found while she waited for deep twilight to descend. When she felt the darkness had grown deep enough to cover her descent she slowly made her way down the steep steps. The rough-cut stone was slick with moisture, forcing her to test her footing before she placed her full weight on each step, or else risk a possibly fatal tumble to the cliff's bottom.

When at last she reached the last step she heaved a sigh of relief. Dogma sniffed the air and gave Sydney a questioning look. "Don't worry, girl, we'll find him. And then we're getting out of here, I promise."

She was happy to see that the only street in Graceville was empty. Other than Ferret Face, and the man who had taken Jordan away, she'd seen only a couple other people moving about the town.

Sydney headed for the large garden she had spied from the wall above and released the chickens to scratch for food in the greenery. The happy hens squawked and fluttered their wings, then raced into the garden.

Sydney hoped she would be able to round them up after she found Jordan, but she couldn't waste time worrying about that now. The birds needed to eat and her priority was finding Jordan as soon as possible.

She hid her backpack inside a large plastic barrel that stood near the garden and pulled her crossbow and several bolts from it. She checked and patted her knife sheath and placed the bolts in the special quill sewn onto her right pant leg.

She said a silent prayer that she wouldn't have to use any weapons tonight. She desperately wanted the killing to be behind her.

Sydney stared out over the black lake. Only a small portion of the surface reflected what little moonlight came down through the light hole. The mass of black water with its unseen far shore gave Sydney an uneasy feeling. The water's opacity felt menacing, as if unknown dangers lurked beneath it's solid surface, waiting to snag any unsuspecting creatures that ventured too close.

She shivered and buried her free hand in Dogma's ruff for assurance. The great dog seemed to sense her need and pushed against Sydney's hip.

"I'm so glad you're with me, girl," whispered Sydney. She turned her back on the lake and hurried toward the center of Graceville where the brick building with the barred windows waited for her. Somehow she knew that was where she'd find Jordan.

Sydney quietly passed by two of the clumsily built shanty shacks. No sound came from either. It was impossible to tell if the inhabitants were asleep or not at home.

As she approached the third shack she heard a woman's voice inside. She pressed up close to the shack's side wall and waited. The woman's voice sounded happy, realized Sydney. The woman chortled and spoke rapidly. Sydney listened for an answering voice but heard only the one female speaking.

She moved soundlessly along the shack's wall and peered around the corner. Full night had fallen and there was no light to see by. Even the faint moonlight had vanished. She waited and listened for several minutes.

The one-sided conversation picked up again and grew louder. The speaker now sounded as if she were arguing, but Sydney still couldn't hear a second person.

She took advantage of the argument and moved along the front of the shack as quickly as possible. She had almost reached the opposite corner when she felt and heard a door squeak open beside her. A person came through the door and plowed into Sydney, knocking her off balance.

Sydney stumbled but managed to regain her footing. Now what? Would the woman alert the town to her presence? Should she knock the woman down and gag her? She waited, muscles tensed, for the woman to scream.

"Are you stupid? I must see the king," muttered the woman. "Not fair. I like pink, not red. Must tell the king." She shuffled off into the darkness.

What was that all about? Sydney wondered. What king? The woman was definitely agitated about something. She wondered why the woman hadn't screamed, or at the very least, gasped, when she ran into Sydney. If their roles were reversed Sydney would've been startled and probably frightened out of her wits.

She hesitated only a moment before deciding to follow the woman. Although she couldn't see a blessed thing in the total darkness, she could hear the woman talking not far ahead. She hurried to catch up and followed as close as she dared until she heard a door open and close. The muttering abruptly stopped.

Sydney stood in the street poised for flight. Did someone else come into the street, or had the woman entered a building?She felt for Dogma. There was no tension in her companion's massive body. Sydney relaxed. Dogma would've been on high alert if there had been any indication of danger.

She took several steps in the direction of the door but stopped short when she stubbed her toe on an unseen obstacle. Cursing softly, she leaned down and felt a small jumble of rough bricks. How had the woman moved so quickly in the dark?

While she had waited for sunset atop the cliff earlier Sydney had noticed that the asylum was surrounded with loose brick and debris. The same debris that now lay at her feet. The woman had led her straight to Jordan.

Sydney carefully slid a foot forward, looking for the path the woman must have taken through the piles of debris, and slowly made her way to the entrance.

She hesitated at the door. Would there be a guard? She searched the building's facade and saw no lights burning inside. She and Dogma would be safe entering the asylum in the dark, she reasoned, although it would make the search for Jordan that much more difficult.

She reached out, felt for the door handle, and pulled gently. The door was heavier than she expected and required both hands to pull open. She let herself in with Dogma close on her heels. The door clicked tightly closed behind them.

If possible, the darkness seemed even more intense inside

the building. Sydney held her breath and heard the woman's footsteps above her, climbing a set of stairs. There were two floors to search. How could she possible find Jordan in this large building in total darkness? More worrying, her crossbow was useless without light to see her target.

Sydney's unease grew. It wouldn't do for both of them to be captured. It had been stupid for her to come in the dark. She debated staying or turning back and waiting for first light. As if in response to her sudden anxiety, Dogma stuck her nose in Sydney's hand.

Relief swept through Sydney. Of course. Dogma could find Jordan by smell, even in the dark. There was no reason for her to panic. They would all soon be away from this place.

She bent her head down close to Dogma's face and whispered in her ear. "Find Jordan, Dogma. Find Jordan."

She grabbed hold of Dogma's ruff and willed the great beast to lead her to Jordan. Dogma sniffed the floor, then surged forward. "Easy, girl," whispered Sydney. "I can't move that fast in the dark."

She tugged gently on Dogma's fur to reinforce her words. To her relief Dogma slowed, but Sydney could feel her desire to race forward. Good. It meant that Jordan was now, or at least had once been, in the building. She hoped she would not have to search the rest of the town for her friend.

Dogma led Sydney to a staircase and they began to climb. Sydney counted eight steps before they reached a landing. She tugged Dogma to a halt and listened but heard nothing from the floor above. They climbed ten more steps and met with another metal door.

Sydney groped for the door handle and opened the heavy door cautiously. She poked her head through and listened again. This time she heard faint voices from down the hall.

She wrapped her hand gently around Dogma's muzzle, the signal to be silent, and then urged the dog through the door, closing it quietly behind them.

According to the floor plan she had studied in the town office, they were in a hallway, one of two on each floor of the asylum. The private patient rooms lined both sides of the halls, twenty rooms per hall. The first floor had crumbled under the weight of the building when it fell through the light hole, so there were only two floors now. That meant there were eighty possible rooms to search for Jordan.

The good news was that she wouldn't have to enter every room; she only needed to let Dogma sniff at each door.

Sydney moved forward, careful not to make a sound, dragging one hand along the wall and holding tight to Dogma with the other. The hand on the wall met open space and she stopped abruptly, feeling across the opening. Either the door was open, or it had been removed.

Hearty snores flowed from the room. Dogma expressed no interest in the occupant so they moved on.

The next door also stood open. Sydney felt along the door jamb and found empty hinges. All of the doors had been removed. That would make it easier for Dogma to smell the occupants, but it also meant there was a greater chance of being heard and discovered as she moved down the hallway. Her boots made noise, but she refused to remove them again. She would have to step very softly.

Sydney slowed her steps and set each booted foot on the floor with deliberate precision. Slow Walking inside, she thought wryly. She was learning that the hunting techniques Smokey had taught her could be used under almost any circumstances.

They checked four rooms. Dogma showed no interest in any of the occupants. They made their way to the fifth room and stood in the doorway. Dogma again showed no interest and Sydney turned to leave.

"Are you the Ghost of Christmas Future?" whispered a thin, reedy voice.

Sydney jumped and turned back toward the room. "What?"

"Cause if you are then I have some requests to make," continued the voice, ignoring her. "I wasn't real thrilled with the Ghost of Christmas Past, I can tell you that. I never got what I wanted no matter how well I behaved. And Christmas Present hasn't bothered to show up in years. So if you're the Ghost of Christmas Future I'm placing my order now. I'd like a canon, a big, black, shiny canon, and I'll need a pile of balls to go with it."

Sydney's curiosity overcame her compulsion to run. She took a small step into the room. "Why do you want a canon? That's a rather odd Christmas gift, isn't it?"

"Are you stupid? That's what my father always said when I made out my wish list for presents." The voice dropped in timbre. "That's an odd thing to ask for, son." Sydney realized the speaker was mimicking his parent.

The voice returned to its thin reediness. "I never got anything I asked for." The man sighed and sounded dejected, then his voice brightened. "But I know you'll bring me a canon. I'm going to launch myself to the far side of the lake you see. I'm a great explorer and we explorers sometimes have to use extraordinary means to reach our goals."

"Ahhh, of course," said Sydney, stepping back out of the room. "I will see what I can do for you. What is your name, so I can be sure to bring the canon to the right person?"

"Thank you, Ghost of Christmas Future. Thank you very, very much. I am called Sir Lewis and Clark."

Sydney furrowed her brow. "Sir Lewis *and* Clark? That

seems a little odd." She stopped. What was she saying? She was standing in an asylum in the middle of the night pretending to be the Ghost of Christmas Future for crying out loud. There were bound to be a few oddballs in the building. She smiled, glad the room's occupant couldn't see her in the dark.

"I must be on my way. More people to visit, you know." She started down the hall, hesitated a moment, and returned to the room. "Sir Lewie, I hope you don't mind if I call you that. I am looking for someone who is a new arrival. His name is Jordan."

"Oh—I've never had a nickname before. I'm not sure about that. Would you be the only one to use it?"

"Absolutely," replied Sydney. "Only the Ghost of Christmas Future can call you Sir Lewie. Have you seen Jordan?"

"You speak of the court's new minstrel. A very fine young knight that Sir Jordan is. The king is very pleased with his gift of the new royal staff."

Sydney's heartbeat quickened. "Can you tell me where to find Sir Jordan? It is very important that I speak with him. I need to, ah, clarify a request he made." Sydney held her breath.

"What can you possibly want with Sir Jordan?" The whisper took on a scornful tone. "He is not in need of anything. He is not a great explorer like me, he is only a lowly entertainer, and not even as talented as the king himself. Don't waste your time on him. Good night, Ghost of Christmas Future. I will expect your gift within the week."

Sydney started to protest that Christmas was several months away, but stopped herself. She tried to think of a way to get the information she sought from Sir Lewis and Clark, but immediately gave up. There was no point in using reason on an unreasonable person.

She continued down the hall, checking each room and moving on when Dogma displayed no interest. They soon covered the entire second floor without finding any sign of Jordan.

Sydney felt her way back to the stairwell and climbed to the third floor but found the door to the hall locked. She made her way back down to the second floor and tried the stairs at the opposite end of the hall. The third floor doors were locked there as well.

She pressed her ear against the metal door and listened. She heard several voices, too faint to make out the words. In spite of the danger of being discovered, she sat on the steps and debated what to do next. The woman Sydney had followed would have simply knocked and gained entry, but that wasn't something Sydney dared to try.

She leaned against the wall and closed her eyes, suddenly overwhelmed with fatigue and the difficulty of the situation. It had been a very, very long day.

The barefoot trek through the cavern as she followed Jordan and his captor to Graceville had seemed to take an eternity, or at the very least, several stressful hours. Finding the access hole and searching the town above, and then searching this building in the dark had sapped the remainder of her energy.

She shouldn't have sat down, she realized. Her body might refuse to get up again. Her eyelids drooped. She couldn't fight it any longer, she had no reserves left. Sydney fell asleep.

Sometime later the door crashed open behind her and jolted her awake. A body tripped over her outstretched legs.

"Are you stupid?" cried a woman.

Sydney recognized the voice. It belonged to the woman she had followed from the shanty. "Sorry. I didn't mean to trip you up. Are you all right?" The woman ignored her. She descended the stairs, muttering about lipstick and pink.

Sydney realized she hadn't heard the door latch behind the woman. She scrambled to her feet and grabbed it before it locked her out. She waited a moment, heard no one on the other side, and stuck her head through the opening to listen for a guard.

Sensing no one close by, she eased through the doorway with Dogma and stood quietly, waiting to see if anyone would stop her. Nothing happened.

Sydney moved forward cautiously. A faint flickering light relieved the inky darkness at the far end, but it wasn't enough to penetrate the deep gloom in the hall where Sydney stood.

Goosebumps raised on her arms. The atmosphere felt different on this floor. Other than the man seeking the Ghost of Christmas Future, the rooms below had been filled with peacefully sleeping bodies.

She sensed more agitation and restlessness seeping from the rooms off this hallway.

Dogma felt it too, Sydney thought, as she felt a tremor course along Dogma's back. She put out her hand and felt her way along the wall until she reached the first room door. This time she found an actual closed door instead of an empty opening.

Dogma didn't even pause to smell at the room. Sydney heard her sniffing the hall floor in an enthusiastic manner. She grabbed Dogma's ruff and let her lead the way down the long hall, pulling the eager dog to a halt when they neared the flickering light at the end of the corridor.

She heard voices from around the corner. A lot of voices.

Walking into the middle of them probably wasn't a smart idea. She needed a plan. Unfortunately she hadn't considered what she would do once she located Jordan.

Sydney pressed against the wall, keeping a tight hold on Dogma. She sniffed the air and realized she smelled woodsmoke. That explained the flickering light; someone had built a fire.

Fortunately the people who had constructed the asylum had built an inflammable building with cement floors and brick walls that wouldn't burn if a patient turned out to be a firebug.

Firebug. Bug. That was the nickname of the man who had set fire to her grandfather's house with Pops inside. One of the men who had raped and killed her twin.

She shook off the memory and stood and listened for Jordan's voice while she tried to understand what the meeting was about. From what she could gather several of the female speakers were engaged in a serious argument over mirrors and lipstick colors.

That explained the shanty woman's agitation over the color pink.

Sydney also heard several male voices, including one that rumbled in an exceptionally smooth and pleasant manner.

The smooth-voiced man began to sing a rocking tune from Sydney's childhood, an old favorite her mother used to dance to whenever it came on the oldies radio station. How her mother had loved that song. She would grab Sydney's and her sister Shannon's hands and lead them, dancing and singing at the top of their voices, through the old farmhouse.

Tears sprang to Sydney's eyes and a sharp pain of longing stabbed through her. She missed her mother and Shannon terribly. They had been more than mother and sister, they had been her closest and most trusted friends. Both now dead. She would never dance and sing with them again.

She dashed the tears from her cheeks and focused on the song. Elvis Presley. Blue Suede Shoes.

"And don't you, step on my blue suede shoes." She sang along in a soft whisper. Another male voice joined the first.

Sydney froze, mouth agape. They had found Jordan and it sounded as if he was having a good time.

The sound of Jordan's voice was too much for Dogma. She pulled away from Sydney's grip, ignored her urgent whispers to come back, and ran around the corner. A sudden silence fell on the third floor. Sydney didn't know whether to stay where she was or follow the dog.

The decision was taken from her when a hand clasped her shoulder. She turned to look at her captor but could only make out a tall dark shadow within the shadows.

"You'd better come with me. The king will want to see you," the shadow said.

7

"Where Do You Come From?" asked the king. His tone sounded far less pleasant now. The king's court all seemed to suck in their breath at once. Jordan heard gasps and frightened whimpers.

"A beast! A beast has entered the court," shrieked a woman.

"Beware the great beast," moaned another.

Jordan's heart galloped in his chest. They could only be referring to Dogma. Which meant that Sydney was somewhere nearby. "My apologies, Your Majesty," he said. "That is my great beast, Dogma. She must have followed me here. She will not harm you unless you threaten me."

Jordan looked around the room anxiously. He recognized Dogma's aura right away. Where was Sydney? A moment later he saw two auras approach the king.

He recognized Sydney's clear, shining colors immediately. They seemed to be attached to an elongated, murky rainbow. Dogma reached his side, pressed against his thigh, and nuzzled Jordan's hand.

He leaned down, gently pulled on her ears, and spoke her

name. He couldn't restrain his smile when she groaned with doggy pleasure. It felt good to have his great beast back by his side.

"Your Majesty," said the elongated aura. "I found this maiden lurking in the hallway. It is obvious she has been sent by a distant kingdom to spy upon us. What shall I do with her?"

"Throw her in the lake!" shouted someone.

"In the lake. In the lake," droned the court.

Sydney looked around the room with interest and trepidation. As she had suspected, a small fire burned on the cement floor in the center of the large space. The fire dried the constant damp that permeated everything below ground and lent an air of cheerfulness to the harsh room.

A wrinkled little gnome of a man pulled a board from a pile that stood to one side and placed it carefully on the fire. The flames popped and burned higher and the room brightened.

Sydney quickly counted twenty or more people gathered around the fire. Jordan stood next to the man they called His Majesty. Dogma sat pressed to Jordan's side, her tongue lolling from her mouth in her expression of doggy nirvana. Sydney knew exactly how she felt. She wished she could press to Jordan's side as well.

Relief washed through her when she saw that other than the purple shadows that underlined the exhaustion in Jordan's bloodshot eyes, he appeared to be unhurt. He had lost his bandage somewhere and the gash over his eye was crusted with dried blood, but she didn't see any sign of swelling or infection.

His majesty, an enormous, dark-skinned man with a head full of tightly curled silver hair, sat in a cracked leather wheelchair and frowned at her. He held Jordan's ram's head staff in one oversized hand. The other rested on his massive thigh.

She saw that the chair arms had been removed to make space for the king's bulk. He wore only a simple loincloth fashioned from a red and white checked fabric that reminded Sydney of a restaurant tablecloth. His immense naked belly obscured most of the cloth.

Sydney realized she was staring with her mouth hanging open. She pressed her lips together to suppress a grin. She had never seen anyone like the man who sat in front of her.

"Where Do You Come From?" repeated his majesty.

The other people in the room stopped moving and stared at her expectantly. Sydney sensed the need for caution with her choice of words; she couldn't risk offending the asylum's residents, especially the man seated in front of her.

Her captor called this man your majesty so she would treat him as if he was true royalty, she decided. She dropped into a deep curtsy. It wasn't as pretty when one was dressed in camouflage pants rather than a dress, but it was the best she could do under the circumstances.

"I am from the land beside the great river, your majesty. I am called...," she hesitated. She needed to sound important so these people would treat her with respect.

Inspiration struck. As a young girl Shanghai Noon had been her favorite movie. She and Shannon had argued over who would play-act Lucy Lui's role. She smiled. "I am Princess Pei-Pei, at your service, your majesty."

A collective gasp sounded around the room.

"She's a princess!"

"A real princess has come to visit the king!"

His majesty inspected Sydney from head to toe and appeared to be satisfied with her claim. "Welcome To My World, Young and Beautiful."

"Welcome, welcome," echoed the king's court.

Sydney inclined her head in a regal manner. "Thank you all, you are very gracious. I apologize for arriving at such a late hour and interrupting your party."

"Party. Party. Party," replied the king.

"Partee, partee!" chorused the court.

"Stranger In My Own Home Town," said the king. He turned his head to look at Jordan. "Mr. Song Man. My Little Friend. My Wish Came True."

"The king's wish came true!" echoed the court. "Truuue! Truuue!"

The king's court reminded Sydney of the Greek chorus in an old Mel Brooks movie. She pursed her lips and surveyed the room. The king sure had a strange way of talking.

She noticed that she and Jordan were not only the youngest people there, other than the king they were the only ones who weren't pale white. These were true cave dwellers. Modern troglodytes.

She realized that everyone's eyes were on her but she didn't sense any danger. At least not at the moment. She needed to keep her wits about her, she reminded herself. Some of these people were possibly killers.

She looked at Jordan and wondered how she could get him alone. "Who is Mr. Song Man, your majesty?" she asked. She needed to know Jordan's status within the group. Was he a prisoner or had he been accepted as one of them?

A petite woman with long, stringy, blonde hair limped awkwardly forward. Despite the fact that she had colored far outside her natural lines when applying scarlet lipstick to her mouth, Sydney could see she had once been attractive. The woman's feet were bare and black with dirt, and her clothing, a navy skirt and suit jacket several sizes too large, hung off her thin frame.

Sydney choked back a gasp and averted her eyes when she realized the woman wore nothing underneath the gaping jacket. No one else seemed to notice anything inappropriate about the woman's attire.

Why would they? thought Sydney as she looked around at the members of the king's court. Everyone there wore something ill-fitting and odd. Their clothing ran the gamut from hospital scrubs, nightgowns and bathrobes, to spandex skirts, blue jeans, and pearl-buttoned cowboy shirts.

She wondered if their clothing had been scavenged from the houses above.

"This is Sir Jordan, the king's new minstrel and my fiancé," the limping woman said proudly. She wrapped her arms around Jordan's neck and kissed him hard on the lips. When she pulled away she left a bright red ring smeared across Jordan's mouth and cheek.

He grimaced and wiped his face with the back of his hand. The king's court clapped and cheered. The king looked pleased.

"Angeline is getting married! Angeline and Sir Jordan sitting in a tree, K-I-S-S-I-N-G!" The court hopped around as they chanted. A few people bounced off one another and several kissed and made smooching noises.

Fiancé? From Jordan's expression Sydney guessed he felt as surprised by the announcement as she did. She watched the gyrating group and wondered if any of the residents of Graceville could legally perform weddings. She sincerely hoped not.

"Earth Angel." The king's smooth, deep voice interrupted Sydney's thoughts.

"Are you talking to me?" Sydney asked, feeling absurdly flattered. No one had ever referred to her as an angel before.

The king focused big brown eyes on her and swept out

his free hand in a curiously graceful movement similar to a hula dancer's move. "Girl Of Mine."

Uh-oh. Suddenly Sydney didn't feel quite so flattered. She had a bad feeling about where this was going. The urge to run was overwhelming, but the king's mesmerizing stare, and the fact that she stood surrounded by the king's court, held her frozen to her spot.

"I Want You, I Need You, I Love You," continued the king. "I'll Never Let You Go."

The king's court broke out in oohs and ahs. Sydney broke out in a cold sweat.

"I Got A Feelin' In My Body. It Feels So Right."

"The king's got a feelin'," chanted the court. "The king wants and loves Princess Pei-Pei. It feels so right."

"I'm So Lonesome I Could Cry," sang the king.

He really did have a beautiful voice, thought Sydney, entranced. But she could not marry the man. She needed to keep moving, needed to find her wise friend Smokey to ask him if she was still worthy of love, or if she had become one of the evil ones and therefore damned herself for all eternity.

She needed to unburden her recent sins, needed to tell someone who knew her before the upheaval–when she was still an innocent–about the men she had killed. Three now.

More importantly, she needed to tell Smokey how she failed to help her sister when Shannon needed her most. Smokey would know if she was doomed. He never lied to her.

"Lonesome king, lonesome king," moaned the court, bringing Sydney back to the present. "He could cry, cry, cry, cry."

Suddenly Sydney understood the king's strange speech pattern. He spoke in song titles. She wondered what he did when he had something to say that had no song to match it. Did he keep the thought to himself? Would it frustrate him?

It was time to take control of the situation, before she found herself married to the loony giant.

Sydney put on a disappointed expression. "Your majesty, I appreciate your feelings, but alas, I am not free to marry you. I am promised to another and must soon be on my way to find him. I came to Graceville because my kingdom has heard wonderful things about you and I wanted to pay my respects. I'm very sorry, but I'm afraid I cannot stay here with you."

The ability to lie came so easy to her now. If her family were still alive they would feel shamed by her glib tongue. What kind of woman had she become? How much of herself would she have to lose in order to survive?

She waited anxiously to see how the king would respond to her answer. The king's court stopped gyrating and frowned and scowled at her in silence. Sydney wondered if she had made a tactical error in refusing the king's attentions. Perhaps she should have gone along with his majesty until she found a chance to sneak away.

"Heart Of Stone. Help Me Make It Through The Night." The king continued to hold her captive with his melodious voice and unwavering stare. He reached a beseeching hand toward her and his expressive eyes grew very sad.

Sydney felt an almost uncontrollable urge to weep. The king should have been an actor. She wondered about his life before the asylum. Why had his family committed him? He was obviously a very talented man.

"Heart of Stone. Heart of Stone." The court's chant became angry. A great wave of tension and animosity rolled toward Sydney. The unfeeling princess had displeased their king. Off with her head!

Sydney forced herself to stand erect and regal, just as she imagined a real princess would behave in the face of danger. She kept her focus on the large man in front of her and tried to ignore the angry mutterings of the others. How dangerous were they? Other than the bow her captor had taken from her, they held no weapons that she could see, but an angry mob could inflict a lot of damage, even kill, with their bare hands.

The king spread his fingers toward Sydney. His voice grew low and intimate, almost a whisper. "I Beg You. I Can't Stop Loving You."

Nonplussed, Sydney stood silent and stared into the king's face. She didn't know what to do to put an end to the situation. Would the king and Angeline want a double wedding? She looked at Jordan and found him staring her way, his eyes steely gray.

She swallowed and tried to come up with some way to dissuade the king from wanting her. Apparently it didn't matter that she was betrothed to another. Perhaps the king saw through her and knew that she had lied. Before she could speak, Jordan turned and bowed toward the king.

"Your Highness, perhaps it is time to tell you the whole truth about me. It is true that I am a minstrel and a musician much like yourself. I have traveled the world with Princess Pei-Pei giving concerts to other great rulers and dignitaries."

Jordan turned toward Sydney. "The Princess is my wife. On our way here we became separated in the great cavern and I was lost until Sir William found me and brought me to you. So you see, we cannot marry you and Angeline because we are already married—to each other. Bigamy is against the law of the land, as you know."

Sydney's mouth dropped open in surprise. She hastily snapped it shut. Apparently lies came easily to Jordan as well.

She hadn't expected that of him, but now she realized that she should have. Since hooking up with him, Jordan James had been a constant source of surprises.

She looked anxiously back toward the king. Would his majesty buy Jordan's story after she had just told him she was on her way to marry someone else? She prayed that he would; Jordan had created a brilliant excuse for them to decline both Angeline's and the king's affections.

Nerves made her taut as a cocked bowstring as she watched the king and waited for his response. The court stood unnaturally silent as they also waited for their ruler's decision. It felt as though everyone had stopped breathing.

At last the king smiled and shrugged. "Easy Come, Easy Go," he said.

Sydney's knees shook and she almost collapsed with relief.

"Easy come, easy go!" shouted the court. They began hopping about the fire again, chanting,"go, go, go."

Sydney was jostled out of her spot in front of the king. She took advantage of the opportunity and made her way to Jordan's side.

"You okay?" he whispered in her ear as he wrapped an arm around her and pulled her close.

Sydney sagged against Jordan's body, relishing the strength in his arm and broad, hard chest. She nodded and buried her face against his side. Her shoulders shook.

"Syd? What's wrong? Are you crying?" He lifted his free hand to her head and stroked her hair.

Sydney shook her head and lifted her face. Her green eyes danced with merriment. "I'm not crying. I'm laughing. This has to be the most bizarre thing that's ever happened to me," she whispered.

Jordan chuckled and squeezed her. "Agreed, princess.

Let's see if we can get a room to ourselves and make a plan to get out of here."

He turned away from Sydney and spoke quietly to the king. Within minutes one of the king's knights led them to an empty dark room off a different hallway on the same floor.

Sydney groped her way along the room's wall until she tripped over a low, narrow bed. She sat on it and leaned back against the wall. Exhaustion hit her hard. Her mind was spinning. It had been a long, long, long, extremely trying day.

She called to Jordan and helped him settle next to her. He sat back against the wall with a heavy sigh. His arm and leg pressed against hers, giving off a welcome heat. Dogma lay on the floor at their feet. It was a relief to be together again.

"So, tell me about your day," she said, affecting the tone of a normal housewife greeting her husband after a day at the office. "And don't leave out anything."

Jordan told her about the green and blue knights and how the king thought he was Elvis Presley but behaved like a real king.

"Did you notice the king's speech?" asked Sydney. "He speaks in song titles."

"Not just any song titles," Jordan replied with a chuckle. "According to Sir Thomas he only speaks in Elvis Presley song titles. Apparently the king has memorized all four hundred plus songs that Elvis ever performed. It's an amazing feat, when you think about it. I don't know how he does it but he manages to get his thoughts across."

Sydney groaned. "He certainly made it clear that he wanted to marry me. Telling him we were already married was quick thinking on your part. I owe you. You should see his majesty. He is rather…majestic."

"In what way?"

"He has this beautiful dark skin and curly silver hair and looks like an old sumo wrestler. Honest–the guy is humongous. He does have a lovely voice though, doesn't he? And his eyes are incredibly expressive. I wonder why he ended up in the asylum, he seems harmless."

They sat in quiet companionship for several minutes. Sydney leaned her head against Jordan's arm and began to doze off.

"Sir Thomas claims the asylum inmates got rid of the staff who were unlucky enough to be in the building when it fell into the sinkhole," said Jordan quietly.

Sydney's eyes popped open. "That's not good. I found quite a bit of information about the asylum in the town hall above. Apparently one section housed dangerous inmates: people who had killed and then claimed insanity in their defense. I suspect they're the ones who killed the staff. I thought the ones with the king tonight were harmless, but who can tell? They're all at least a little out of touch with reality."

"I believe Sir Thomas is one of the dangerous ones," said Jordan. "There's something menacing about his aura. When I first talked with him it looked brighter than the others so I assumed he wasn't quite as bad off, but when he talked about the staff his aura changed. It grew dark and chaotic and felt angry."

Jordan felt for Sydney's hand and laced his fingers through hers. "I can't tell you how happy I felt to see a clear aura in the room. I knew it had to be yours even before I heard your voice. Did you have any trouble finding me?"

Sydney burrowed under Jordan's arm and leaned her head against his chest. The sound of his strong heartbeat sounded soothing. "I almost lost you in the cavern until you started singing."

She remembered how the darkness had solidified into a living entity, one that invaded her body and squeezed the breath from her lungs.

She rubbed Dogma gently with the toe of her boot. "I was sure Dogma would find you, so I wasn't too worried, but I hated walking alone in the dark. I don't know how you do it." She felt him raise his shoulder in a shrug.

"People do what they have to do, I guess. I can't spend the rest of my life sitting in one spot. As you well know since you saved me from starving to death."

Jordan tightened his arm around Sydney's slim shoulders. It felt wonderful to have her with him again. The more time they spent together the more determined he became not to let the mysterious Smokey have her.

He knew that something troubled her deeply. He also knew that she had courage and intelligence and integrity. He wished he could convince her to trust him and share whatever ate at her soul.

She had told him about the two men she had killed to protect her grandfather. What more could there be? Jordan knew that he could accept whatever she had done. More importantly, he could find a way to help her.

Fatigue overtook them and they fell silent. Jordan lay down against the wall and Sydney lay next to him. They barely fit together on the narrow bed, but she nestled her back against his chest and tucked her bottom into his groin.

He laid his arm over her and held her tight. *If only we weren't both so tired I might be able to take advantage of the situation. It* was his last waking thought. Sydney was already asleep.

Dogma's soft growls woke them near dawn. A faint gray light filled the room's only window. Dogma was on her feet, pressed tight against the bed, facing the door. Her chest rumbled with a deeper, louder growl.

"What is it, girl?" asked Jordan softly. He heard the room door softly open. He raised his head to see over Sydney's shoulder and saw an aura standing there. This aura was clearer than the one's belonging to the members of the king's court, with only a hint of murkiness around the edges. He recognized it as belonging to his unwelcome fiancée. She stood in the doorway and waited.

"Who's there?" asked Jordan, his voice firm and authoritative. He felt Sydney tense against him and knew she was awake.

The aura took a step into the room. "It's Angeline, Sir Jordan. I must speak with you."

"Dogma, stay. You may enter, Angeline. Dogma will not hurt you unless I command her to. What do you want?"

The aura took another step closer. "I want you to take me away from here," answered Angeline. "I'm not like the others. I don't belong here."

8

"COME in and tell us why you want to leave, Angeline," said Sydney. She sat up and moved to the edge of the bed and put her feet on the floor. "Why do you say you don't belong here?"

Angeline moved further into the room but stayed a healthy distance from Dogma. "I'm not a patient. I was one of the staff. The sinkhole opened up and swallowed the asylum on my second day on the job. I was trapped in a pile of rubble."

"Is that how you hurt your leg?" asked Sydney. The poor woman. Her second day on the job and she ends up falling into a sinkhole with a building full of people suffering from mental illnesses. What were the odds? Talk about bad karma.

Angeline nodded. "My leg broke in the fall. It's never been set properly so it healed crooked. But it saved my life. That and the fact that very few of the inmates knew my face because I was so new. I was still buried in the rubble when Sir Thomas and his friends killed the rest of the staff. When they found me and dug me out they assumed I was another patient. After they told me the staff was dead I kept my mouth shut and pretended to be a new patient."

"It must have been awful for you," said Sydney. "I can't imagine the strain you've been living under trying to fit in with the other patients."

Some of the tension eased from Angeline's body. She lowered herself to the floor. "My real name is Bethany Jane. How did you end up here? Did you fall into a sinkhole too?"

Sydney shook her head. "Nope. We fell down a cliff and got stuck in the Nebraska desert. I found a cave and we decided to see where it led since we couldn't climb back up the cliff." She shrugged. "And here we are."

Jordan had joined Sydney on the edge of the bed while the women were talking. He searched Angeline/Bethany's aura and tried to understand what it told him. Her aura was not as clear and bright as Sydney's; there were several areas where the colors were off and muddied, but it looked much clearer than the others he had observed in the asylum.

He wondered if Angeline/Bethany was starting to believe the role she was playing—that would explain the mixed aura.

"Do you know how to get back to the surface?" he asked.

"Yes. There's an access hole that Sir Henry uses when he scavenges the old town. We can use it to get out of here."

"Let's say we climb to the surface," said Jordan. "We'll still be stuck in the desert with no water source and who knows how far to travel before we find some." He shook his head. "I'm not sure we'd be better off. At least down here there's water to drink."

Angeline/Bethany scowled. "Are you saying you want to stay in Graceville? I've had enough of these loonies. I want out. You two can help me. Once I find a new place to live you can leave me."

"Us three," corrected Sydney. "Don't forget Dogma. She

goes where we go. That means the access hole is out. She can't climb a rope ladder."

Angeline/Bethany's scowl deepened. "Are you stupid? You'd stay here because of a stupid dog?"

Sydney pursed her lips. She didn't care for the other woman's attitude toward Dogma. The great beast was smarter and more loyal than most people. They would never leave her behind.

"What's with the "are you stupid" bit that I keep hearing?" interrupted Jordan. "Everyone says it."

Angeline/Bethany waved a dismissive hand. "The asylum had an orderly who thought it was funny to ask everyone if they were stupid, It didn't matter if they were patients or staff, he did it to everybody. I only knew him one day and I found him to be really obnoxious. I don't know why, but the patients say it all the time now."

"You just said it yourself," Sydney pointed out.

Angeline/Bethany looked surprised, then scowled. "I did? You see? I really need to get out of here or I'm going to end up just like them."

"What can you tell us about the king?" asked Jordan.

A wistful expression came over Angeline/Bethany's face. "He's magnificent, isn't he? The woman who was training me said his parents had him committed in his late teens. I think he's in his forties now. She said he took a bad mix of hallucinogenics and some other drugs at an Elvis Presley concert and he never recovered."

"He has an incredible voice and way about him. He could've been a professional singer," said Sydney. "He's almost mesmerizing."

"I agree. I'll miss him terribly when I leave. He's a fascinating man." Angeline/Bethany stood. "I'd better get back to the court. Keep calling me Angeline in front of the others, please. If Sir Thomas ever learns that I was staff he'll kill me too. I'll be in touch to make plans for our escape."

She cracked the door and checked the hallway, then let herself out of the room, closing the door quietly behind her.

The light in the window grew brighter. Sydney looked around the room. It was bare except for the hard, unwelcoming bed. The concrete walls were battered and scuffed and painted a vile shade of acid green. A single empty light fixture hung from the center of the ceiling.

No attempt had been made to make the space pleasant or appealing or something other than institutional. If a person wasn't already unbalanced the room's decor would drive them crazy. She shivered and turned to Jordan.

"Well, what do you think? Is Angeline/Bethany being truthful with us? And if she is, do we want to take her with us when we leave?"

"I don't know. Her aura is growing muddy around the edges, so living here is definitely taking a toll on her sanity. The question is, can she revert to who she was before, or has she changed too much to fit in with the, quote, normal, unquote, world? I'm not sure we'd be doing her any favors by taking her away from Graceville."

"If we don't find a way out of here it won't matter one way or another," said Sydney. "We'll all end up with muddy auras and spend our nights dancing around a fire and echoing the king. Then I'll be forced to find a cannon for Sir Lewis and Clark."

"What?"

Sydney told him about being mistaken for the Ghost of Christmas Future. Jordan barked out a laugh and she found herself grinning in spite of their predicament. She was about to suggest they leave the building and make their way to the access hole when a knock came on the door.

"Who is it?" called Jordan in a stern voice. He wanted whoever stood on the opposite side of the door to think twice before entering. He felt a strong need to create boundaries between the asylum inmates and himself and Sydney. It was a small step toward exerting control over their situation.

The door flew open with a loud bang. Dogma growled at the wiry man with ginger colored hair as he stepped into the room with a snappy salute.

"Sir Jordan and Princess Pei-Pei, your presence is required in the king's chamber A-S-A-P. That means as soon as possible in case you didn't know." Pride for possessing that tidbit of knowledge flashed on his face. "I am to escort you there."

The messenger gave Dogma a wary look. "And the great beast as well." He turned sharply, stepped outside the room, and stood at soldierly attention.

"Guess we have to see what the king wants. Maybe it's breakfast time," said Jordan, ever hopeful of a good meal. He stood and felt for Sydney's shoulder, then ran his hand down her arm to her hand. Grasping it firmly, he pulled her to her feet. "Come along, princess. The king awaits our presence."

Their escort refused to answer any questions, leading them in silence through the halls to the king's chamber. Several men stood at stiff attention outside the chamber and glared at them as they passed by. Their animosity was palpable.

A warning tingle passed through Sydney's body. She balked and tried to turn back but the men fell into place behind her and pushed them through the door. She swore under her breath. Something had definitely changed since their earlier audience with the king.

She followed the escort through the doorway and stopped. The room held twice as many people as it had during her first visit, but the chamber was strangely quiet. She led Jordan into the room, Dogma at his side, and made her way through the crowd toward the king's chair.

His highness sat with his back to her, facing the main group. Sydney recognized several of the dancers and smiled at them, but none smiled in return. In fact everyone looked quite puzzled in a grim way. No, they look in shock, she realized.

Whatever the situation, it had to be bad for her and Jordan.

"Good morning, Your Highness," she said to the king's back and curtsied. The king did not reply. Were they out of favor with the king already? wondered Sydney. Why didn't he turn around and face them?

When she stood back up she noticed a man she hadn't seen the night before standing beside the king, staring at her. The man's facial expression worried her. It held a mixture of anger and triumph, but it was the sadistic gleam in his eye that sent a chill of fear down her back. He reminded her of the man she had killed to save her grandfather. Too late, as it had turned out.

She pushed the memory from her mind, swallowed her fear, and tried to look princess-like and unruffled as she cooly held the man's stare. She felt anything but cool. Her heart beat so hard she feared she might suffer a heart attack.

"My name is Sir Thomas, Princess Pei-Pei," said the man. "The king and his court are my prisoners. As are you and Sir Jordan."

Sydney felt Jordan's body tense beside her. She squeezed his fingers to let him know he shouldn't try any heroics. She knew Sir Thomas wouldn't hesitate to hurt or kill at the slightest provocation; she could see it in his eyes. This was the man who set people on fire and killed innocent staffers. He was bad news of the worst sort.

"Why would you take the king prisoner, Sir Thomas?" she asked. Her voice wobbled a little and she steadied it. "Are you qualified to rule in his place? If you are then perhaps you should employ the same method our country uses to determine leadership and hold an election."

Jordan watched Sir Thomas's aura flare. He squeezed Sydney's hand to let her know she should shut up before Sir Thomas lost control. He had caught hints of Sir Thomas's madness the night before. Now he clearly felt the dark evil emanating from the knight.

Sir Thomas's laugh held no humor. He turned the king's wheelchair around and stood beside it again.

Sydney gasped. The king had been gagged, his meaty hands tied to his thighs, his thighs lashed to the chair. She saw a deep sadness in his eyes as he looked at her. He reminded her of a polar bear she had seen in a small zoo once. A magnificent wild creature who had been confined in a cage too small.

"Why have you gagged the king?" she demanded. "Surely he cannot hurt you with his voice?"

Sir Thomas flicked the king's skull with a finger. "I'm sick to death of him talking in Elvis Presley song titles. What kind of man talks that way? He should speak like a normal man, for crying out loud. For over twenty years now I've been listening to those same phrases over and over. He's making me crazy."

Sydney stared at Sir Thomas in disbelief. "I beg your pardon? Making you crazy? I think, Sir Thomas, that you have achieved that all on your own. You do live in an asylum after all. The king is harmless. Stay away from him if you don't want to listen to him talk. There's no reason to stage a coup."

"Coo, Coo," whispered the king's followers.

Sir Thomas glared at them and they fell into a fidgety silence. Sydney felt sympathy for them. This was a group that could not be still for long. They let out the stresses of their mental illness in constant movements.

She looked for Angeline and found her in the middle of the group, staring at the king with tears in her eyes. She really cares for the king. Sydney's opinion of Angeline rose.

Sir Thomas focused his stare on Sydney and pursed his lips. For several minutes everyone waited in silence to see what he would do. She grew worried when she saw a sudden gleam come into his eyes. Whatever he had come up with couldn't be good. She hoped he wouldn't hurt the king in retaliation for her rash words.

"I'll tell you what," Sir Thomas said finally. "You are obviously fond of his highness here. Marry me and I'll set the king free."

"Free, free!" echoed the court a little louder this time.

Sydney blinked. And blinked again. She couldn't find her tongue. She stared at the chinless, sneering man in front of her and tried to think. There had to be a way out of this mess.

"Marry? Uh, I cannot, Sir Thomas. I'm already married to Sir Jordan." She lifted Jordan's hand, still holding her own. The lie had dissuaded the king last night, maybe it would work on Sir Thomas.

Sir Thomas's dark eyes grew hooded. "No problem, Princess. I can make you a widow easily enough, or Sir Jordan can live and we can live together in sin. I have my own place you know. You won't be living in the palace with the crazy people."

"What a tempting offer. I've always wanted a place of my own." She had trouble keeping the sarcasm from her voice.

Sydney looked over the crowd, searching for the tall, thin man who had escorted her into the king's chamber last night. She spied him near the left edge of the court, the crossbow pistol he had taken from her still slung over his shoulder.

She breathed a sigh of relief. No one had thought to take the bolts from the quiver attached to her thigh. She only needed to get her crossbow back and she'd be able to put a quick end to this little coup of Sir Thomas's.

"I think I need a little time to make my decision," Sydney said, creasing her forehead to make it look as if she was thinking hard. "You're asking me to make a major, life-changing choice. Could you give me twenty four hours?"

If Sir Thomas held her and Jordan captive with the others she'd be set. It made sense for him to keep all of his prisoners together in the king's chamber, she reasoned. It made controlling them easier. Confident of her reasoning, she gave Sir Thomas a small smile. This nightmare would all be over with in no time.

"Certainly, Princess," answered Sir Thomas with a bow. "I understand your difficulty. This presents a fine opportunity to be rid of your husband and start anew. You may have twenty four hours, starting now. We will wait here for your return."

Return? He was sending her out of the room! For crying out loud, couldn't any of these people think or act in a logical manner?

Sydney inclined her head and thanked Sir Thomas, then squeezed Jordan's hand. "I'll be back," she whispered and started for the door.

"One thing before you go, Princess," said Sir Thomas. "If

you are not back here within twenty four hours I will kill Sir Jordan and the king."

Sydney turned and frowned. "How will you know when the twenty four hours are up—there are no clocks here."

Sir Thomas shrugged. "That's the tricky part. I suggest you return early."

9

SYDNEY WASTED NO TIME. She dashed from the king's chamber. She needed to make a plan, one that would liberate the king and his followers as well as Jordan, and preferably one that didn't involve bloodshed.

She returned to the gardens to check on Ginny and Henrietta. The hens were happily scratching up greens and bugs so she left them there. She grabbed her backpack from the plastic barrel and made her way back to the cliff steps and the access hole. Something told her that any hope she had of defeating Sir Thomas would be found in the town above.

Climbing the rope ladder with her pack took most of Sydney's remaining strength. Her arms and legs trembled from the effort. Several times she was forced to stop and hook her arms through the ladder and simply hang, panting, while she gathered enough strength to continue on.

Once she missed the rung with her foot and slipped. She hung by her hands for what seemed an eternity while she frantically searched for a foothold. The pack felt like an elephant hanging on her back, dragging her toward the ground. Her shoulders screamed in protest and the rope burned her fingers as she willed herself not to let go.

At the moment she knew she couldn't hold on any longer her right toe grabbed hold of the rung. She released a sob of relief and quickly placed her left foot beside the right. It took several minutes before she felt able to free her cramped hands from the ladder.

Sydney leaned her forehead against the dirt wall of the access hole and waited for her ragged breathing to smooth out. I can't do this. I'm not strong enough.

But what were her options? She had no choice. She had to find a way to defeat Sir Thomas or Jordan would die.

She took a deep breath and resumed the climb. She gave a weak shout of victory when she reached the top, pulled herself onto the hot, dry surface and lay gasping in the sun. When her racing pulse slowed to a normal pace she stood and stumbled toward the town.

She made her way past the house with the tumbleweed, (wasn't she just here?), past the streets of modest homes, to Main Street and the municipal building. She needed to eat to replenish her energy and then come up with a rescue plan. The town office was the safest place to do all of that.

She caught movement from the corner of her right eye, but when she turned to face it there was nothing there. She quelled the cold shudder of fear that ran down her spine.

"I'm hallucinating," she muttered to herself. "It's just tumbleweed. This may be a ghost town but there is no such thing as ghosts. Buck up, Sydney girl. You still have to save an asylum full of lunatics and find a way to escape the aquifer that doesn't involve dying in the desert."

She forced herself to start walking again. Her current situation was as serious as any she had ever faced.

The town hall felt cool and welcoming. Sydney removed

her pack and made her way to the storeroom where she had earlier found the government food rations. Most of the use-by dates on the cans had expired, but she found several that showed no sign of spoilage.

She opened a can of beef stew but after inspecting the contents she decided not to eat it. The last thing she needed was food poisoning. She opened a package of freeze-dried chicken soup instead and retrieved her water bottle from her pack. Cold freeze-dried soup did not make a very tasty meal, but she made herself force it down. She needed the energy from the calories.

She was forcing down a second package of soup when she heard the building's entrance door open and close. Sydney scrambled to her feet and pulled her knife. A wave of dizziness washed over her and she leaned against the pile of cartons to steady herself.

I don't have time for this. She willed the weakness to pass and pushed away from the cartons. She stepped quietly to the open storeroom door and listened, flattened against the wall.

Silence. She slowly poked her head out and looked down the hallway. A man stood at one of the large front windows with his back to her. He looked to be of average height and build and sported a long pony tail. The hair on the right side of his head shone silver white, a sharp contrast to the near black of the hair on his left side.

Sydney didn't dare move lest she attract his attention. Had he seen her?

"I can see your reflection in the window," said the stranger. "What are you doing in my town?" His voice was whispery and raw. It sent a shiver down Sydney's spine.

He turned and faced her. The right half of his face and neck was covered with wide, puckered scars. The right eye drooped and she wondered if he had the use of it. The left side of his face belonged to a once-handsome man.

Sydney stepped out of the room cautiously, holding her knife at her side. She had no way of knowing if this stranger was friend or foe. She prayed he was friendly as she hadn't the strength to defend herself against an enemy.

"My name is Sydney." She sensed this man would not believe she was Princess Pei-Pei. The thought almost made her smile.

"My friend Jordan is being held prisoner inside the asylum by a small group of patients. They have the king also. Who are you?"

She leaned against the wall to hold herself upright. She felt so weak. What was wrong with her?

The man stayed by the window. "My name is Silas. I'm sorry about your friend. If Sir Thomas has him he's probably doomed."

"Don't say that. I have until tomorrow morning to find a way to rescue them. I—."

A swarm of mad hornets buzzed in her head. Everything went black and she slumped to the floor.

Sydney's eyes fluttered open. She found herself staring at unlit florescent ceiling lights. She licked her dry lips and tried to think of the last thing she clearly remembered. Oh yes, Silas with the scarred face. Jordan and the king and Sir Thomas's threats came flooding back.

She turned her head and saw that she was on the store-room floor. Her sleeping bag had been thrown over her body. She rolled to her side and pushed herself to a partial seated position, still trying to clear her fuzzy mind.

"Good, you're awake. I was beginning to worry." The whispery voice came from behind Sydney.

She turned and saw Silas sitting on a Feminine Hygiene carton with his forearms resting on his legs. He watched her carefully.

"How-how long have I been unconscious?" She pulled her legs free of the sleeping bag and pushed herself to her knees. She still felt a little weak, but not as bad as before she passed out.

Silas shrugged. "A couple of hours. You must have been exhausted. Don't try to get up too fast. I don't want you to faint again. You scared the crap out of me."

Panic washed over Sydney. "A couple of hours? I have to get out of here. I have to save Jordan and the king." She stood and tottered a moment, then sat abruptly down again on her bag and held her head. "Maybe I'd better take this a little more slowly," she muttered.

Silas watched her closely with his good eye. He made no effort to hide his disfigurement from her, he faced her straight on. "Do you have a plan?" he asked.

"No. I haven't had time to think about the problem. I came here as soon as Sir Thomas released me and then you showed up and apparently I took a long nap." She frowned at Silas. "I don't suppose you have any ideas."

Silas shrugged one shoulder. "I've had a little time to think while I waited for you to wake up. The problem is I haven't been below for a long time so I don't know what's happening down there."

Sydney moved into a more comfortable cross-legged position and leaned her arms on her thighs.

"The asylum sits in the center of Graceville with approximately two dozen shanties built around it. When I left everyone was confined to the king's chamber. As near as I can tell Sir Thomas only has five men doing his bidding. Unfortunately, even though the rest of the patients vastly outnumber them, they seem unable to organize and overthrow Sir Thomas."

"A slight smile lifted the left corner of Silas's mouth. "Does the king still speak in song titles?"

Sydney nodded and smiled in spite of the seriousness of the situation. "The king is really quite something, isn't he? I've never met anyone like him. How do you know him? I was told he's been living in the asylum for at least twenty years. I feel bad for him. He seems harmless enough."

Silas ignored her question. He leaned against the wall, stretched out his legs and folded his arms across his chest. "I have a score to settle with Thomas. I might be willing to assist you," he said. His good eye glittered with malice.

Glad she wasn't the object of that malice, Sydney stopped smiling, serious again. "I either need help or a very big advantage if I'm going to free my friend and the king and deal with Sir Thomas."

She gestured at his facial scars and grimaced. "Did Sir Thomas do that to you?" She couldn't begin to imagine how painful the experience must have been. From this distance she could see that the scars extended over Silas's neck and under his tee shirt. His arm carried the scars as well.

"Yeah," answered Silas. "Thomas likes to play with fire, especially if it involves pain and suffering for others. I've been living alone up here since the sinkhole opened and everyone left. I'm just waiting for the rest of the town to fall in and put an end to my misery."

Silas fell silent. Sydney waited.

"Helping you could alleviate some of the boredom of waiting. And it would be satisfying to put a hurt on Thomas."

Sydney's spirits rose. Perhaps the situation wasn't as

hopeless as she'd previously thought. "That would be great, I'd appreciate any help you care to give," she said, getting to her feet. "We need weapons of some sort. Are there any left in the town?"

"No, the townspeople took them when they abandoned Farmington. Probably a good thing, otherwise the patients would have them by now. Sir Henry comes through the access hole daily to rummage through the town, that's why I hid the surplus food in these boxes. There's no reason for Henry to look inside them." He gave a ghost of a smile. "Not to worry, I'll come up with something. I have a few ideas," said Silas in his whispery voice.

His good eye held a cold gleam that sent a shiver down Sydney's spine. She crossed her fingers and prayed that asking for Silas's help wouldn't turn out to be a mistake.

Sydney wanted to head right out, but Silas insisted she take the time to eat some of the freeze-dried food packs to build up her energy reserves. The neatly stacked empty cartons she had noticed on her last visit were from him, he told her. He subsisted on the government rations and water left by Sir Henry in exchange for whatever trinkets Silas gave him in return. The lipsticks were from their most recent trade.

She had to admit that she felt much less shaky by the time Silas led her across town to the municipal water tower, a large oval tank suspended on a tall, thin column and painted with rainbow-colored stripes with the town's name printed in faded white across its fat middle.

Sydney craned her neck. "How tall is it?" she asked. Although she had seen water towers from the highways when she used to travel with her father, this was the closest she'd come to one. Standing underneath it the water tank looked immense, its support column impossibly slender.

Silas bent down to inspect something at the base of the support column. "One hundred sixty five feet to the top of the tank," he said as he straightened. "I've removed the nuts and bolts from the base of the support and severed the water pipes inside the center column. Wasn't an easy task, I'll tell you. I've been working on it most every day for the last two years."

He indicated a thin slice in the column's metal skin. "You can see that I've also cut as far into the metal support as I could without having the whole thing crash down on me. Now I just need a way to unbalance the tank and tip it toward the sinkhole. It should make quite a splash."

Sydney frowned. She felt a sharp stab of disappointment. Silas wasn't going to be of any help to her after all. "I don't understand how that will help me free my friend," she said, struggling to sound polite.

A sudden thought hit her. She knew nothing about this man. What if Silas had actually been one of the patients at the mental hospital? The thought paralyzed her.

"What's your plan?" she asked.

Silas gave her his half-smile. The unmarked side of his face glowed with pleasure. "We need a diversion, something Thomas won't be able to ignore. I figure a giant metal object falling from the sky will distract Thomas and his men long enough for us to make our move."

The half-smile took on a wolfish leer. "Especially if the falling object is accompanied by a very large fire. Thomas can't resist fire."

"Maybe you should tell me a little about yourself first, Silas," said Sydney. She was growing more and more concerned about this strange, half-scarred man by the minute. "Just how do you plan to make a large fire?"

Silas grabbed Sydney's arm and led her away from the

water tower. "Have no fear. I wasn't a patient at the asylum if that's what you're wondering," he said, reading her expression. His whisper-voice sounded harsher than usual. He steered her toward a building near the edge of the sinkhole.

"Thomas is my adopted brother," he continued. "He tried to kill me by setting fire to my bed after he tied me to it and gagged me so I couldn't scream. Fortunately my father smelled the smoke and came to investigate. He pulled me free, but not before I sustained second and third-degree burns over one side of my body."

Sydney shuddered. "What a horrid thing to do. Did they commit Thomas to the asylum after that?"

"Not right away. My mother wanted to give him a chance to work through his issues so she placed him in therapy. She felt sorry for Thomas because he'd lost his parents in a house fire. His mother was my mother's sister and she felt responsible for him. Turned out that he had intentionally set the fire that killed his parents. They discovered the truth after I had been in the hospital for almost four months. They committed him to the asylum a short while later."

A cold fear gripped Sydney. Sir Thomas liked to hurt people. There was no way of knowing if he would give her the twenty four hours he promised, or if he would harm Jordan for the sheer fun of it when she returned. She took a deep breath and forced the fear aside. She needed a clear head and worrying about Jordan muddled her brain.

"What can I do to help?" she asked.

They had stopped beside a house on the edge of the sinkhole. Once a modest but roomy home, the back half of the house had fallen into the hole, leaving the remainder leaning and unstable. Silas wrenched opened the front door and ushered Sydney inside a room that ran the width of the structure.

Sydney stood just inside the door, afraid to advance any farther for fear the house would collapse about her ears. She looked questioningly at Silas. "Are you sure it's safe to be in here. What if the sinkhole collapses under us?"

Silas gave her a thoughtful look. "It won't be easy to get at Thomas without somebody getting hurt. My guess is that if we try to rescue your friend without some sort of diversion Thomas will kill him first."

Sydney took a deep breath and nodded. She knew Silas was right. Thomas enjoyed hurting people.

"This house will be our main diversion," continued Silas. "Thomas is obsessed with fire He won't be able to resist it. I want you to gather anything you can find that will burn and fill this room with it. While you do that I'll finish preparations on the water tower."

He turned and strode off before Sydney could speak.

She scavenged loose boards and wooden furniture from the nearest houses first. As she grew accustomed to working around the edge of the sinkhole her fear that the ground would collapse underneath her gradually lessened, although she remained alert for any vibrations.

After getting stuck by several nasty splinters Sydney jogged to the hardware store and found a pair of used gloves stuffed under the counter.

On her way back to the house she spied a wheeled cart with flattened tires. She scavenged a bicycle pump from a backyard shed and soon had the cart functioning. Proud of her accomplishment, she quickly became much more efficient at gathering fuel for the bonfire.

Gradually she filled the front room, tossing boards onto the pile when it became too high for her to merely place them.

The sun had set and the waxing moon was just showing

its face above the eastern horizon by the time Sydney finished her task. She stood in the dusky room and admired her work.

Every muscle in her body ached. Even her eyeballs hurt. But she'd done it. Siding and barn boards, wooden chairs and tables, piles of newspapers and cardboard filled the space. Smiling to herself, she went in search of Silas.

She found him at the water tower, struggling with a length of thick, heavy rope. He had tied one end through the metal ladder and around the center support two thirds of the way up and was dragging the opposite end toward a large farm tractor parked near the edge of the sinkhole.

Sydney grabbed onto the rope and helped Silas pull it to the back end of the tractor. He wrapped it around the back axle several times and tied it off. The tractor loomed over Sydney; the top edge of the rear tires alone stood several feet above her head.

"You have fuel?" She thought of all the vehicles she had walked past on the highways, abandoned to the elements and ever-hungry rust because their owners had run out of fuel.

"I have enough. I've had plenty of time to hide anything I thought I might be needing. Are you finished with the house?"

Sydney assured him she had filled the room with flammables.

"Great. I have one more thing to set up, then we'll take a rest break before we launch our attack. You can either wait for me back at the town hall or meet me at the fire house." Silas took off at a lope without waiting for an answer.

Sydney decided to return to the house. Although she had never been afraid of the dark, tonight she felt uneasy. She told herself it came from not knowing what Thomas would do. For all she knew Thomas might renege on their deal and want her back. Or he could have his minions searching for her.

She refused to admit that her fear of the dark had grown since being stuck in the perpetual night of the aquifer.

Sydney stood outside the house well away from the edge of the sinkhole and looked at the darkening night sky. She found the Big and Little Dippers and the one shaped like a W, the only three constellations she could pick out.

A shooting star flared across the sky and winked out. A good omen, surely? She used to wish upon them with her mother and Shannon. She wished she and Jordan and Dogma were safely beyond Nebraska.

The silence was absolute. It pressed on her from all sides. An intense loneliness washed over Sydney and almost brought her to tears. She missed her parents. She never had the chance to say goodbye to them. She missed her sister Shannon with an ache so fierce it burned in her chest.

She thought of her grandfather, his body walled into the cave where she had left him, and wondered if she would ever return to give him a proper burial.

Everyone she loved gone. Except for Jordan, she reminded herself. Somehow she would save him from Thomas. She couldn't face the alternative. She prayed that Thomas had kept his word and Jordan was still alive. She didn't know how she could go on if she lost him too.

A great roar broke the quiet. Sydney whipped around, ready to flee. Headlights flipped on and she saw a monster-sized earth-moving machine coming toward her. A small gasp escaped her lips. Silas was a very resourceful man, she had to give him that.

She moved to the side and watched Silas drive the huge bulldozer up to the house and stop. He turned off the engine and the silence took over once more.

"Let's go. Time to eat. We'll rest for an hour, then launch our attack," Silas said as he climbed down from the driver's seat. "Thomas won't expect to see you until morning, so by attacking tonight we'll add to the element of surprise. Besides, fire is much more spectacular in the dark."

They returned to the town office storeroom in silence. Silas pulled a candle from his pocket and lit it. The flame cast a welcome light. "I gathered up every candle I could find and hid them from Henry. He never comes in this building for some reason, so anything I want to keep for myself I hide in the basement."

Sydney pulled out several dried packages of food and handed one to Silas. He sat with his burned side away from the light and she marveled at what a handsome man he had once been. Movie star handsome. Women would have hounded him if he'd had the chance to reach manhood before being disfigured.

"What did you do before the upheaval?" she asked. Silas turned his good eye on her. It was a warm brown with gold highlights, she noticed.

"I made furniture," he said. He gestured at the scarred half of his face. "I wanted to be a science teacher, but after this happened I realized I needed to do something that wouldn't necessitate a lot of person-to-person contact. So I made furniture and sold it to a couple shops, let them deal with the customers. What about you?"

"Me? I'd just graduated college. I was going to follow in my father's footsteps and work as a biologist, but the world fell apart right after I got home from school."

Silas nodded. "Tough break. Where's your family now?"

Sydney chewed slowly, giving herself time to manage the pain that pressed on her chest. "My mother was an artist," she said finally. "She was caught in the tsunamis that hit the east coast. She had flown to New York City to attend the gallery opening of a major show centered on her work."

The food in her mouth turned into a dry lump. She forced herself to swallow. "She was only supposed to be gone that one night. Dad was speaking at a meeting for the Fish and Wildlife Service in Yellowstone Park. He never came home either. My sister and I assumed the park went through some major upheavals when the earthquakes started."

She stopped speaking.

Silas looked at her and raised his good eyebrow. "And your sister?" he prodded.

"Shannon was raped and murdered by some wanderers I call The Desperate Ones." She stood and turned her back on Silas while she got her emotions under control. She didn't know why the loss of her family was bothering her so much tonight. She needed to be strong, this was no time for sentimentality.

"I'm so sorry," said Silas, his voice quiet. "That must have been very difficult for you." He sat quietly and gave Sydney time to collect herself.

"Tell me about your friend Jordan," he said after a few minutes. "Will he help us fight against Thomas if it comes to that?"

Having gotten herself under control again, Sydney turned to face Silas. "Jordan will do whatever he can. There's also Dogma, his dog. I call her the great beast. She's intelligent and will also help us. Jordan is blind. But since he's been traveling with me he's developed some interesting skills. He senses inanimate objects fairly accurately, and recently he's started seeing people's auras."

Silas looked surprised, then thoughtful. "How interesting. I've heard stories about handicapped people who develop compensating skills." He flexed the fingers of his burnt hand.

Sydney noticed the fused skin between Silas's fingers and remembered his awkward gait. Of course. Silas was burned on one side of his body, not just his face. His recovery must have been excruciating. Compassion for Silas replaced the pain of her personal losses.

"You may have heard of my friend Jordan," she said aloud. "He was quite a famous musician; played piano and sang all over the world."

Silas's eyebrow shot up. "Are you talking about Jordan James? That's who Thomas is holding prisoner? I used to sing his kind of music, even fancied myself a crooner before the fire."

He gestured at his throat. "Can't sing anymore of course. Too much smoke damage to my vocal chords. But at least I can speak, and I have something to say when I catch up with Thomas." He turned a fierce look upon Sydney that made her glad she wasn't the object of his anger.

What's our plan?" she asked as they put away their trash and settled down to rest. Silas blew out the candles and told her.

Sydney thought she'd be too keyed up to sleep, but the last week had sapped her strength and she fell into a restless doze almost immediately. She dreamt of Shannon and her grandfather and the men she had killed and of an innocent man tied to his bed and set afire.

"Sydney, wake up." Silas shook her shoulder gently.

Sydney gasped and sat up. She saw they were still in the storeroom and she closed her eyes for a moment while the last wisps of the dreams dissipated.

"Time to go," said Silas.

SYDNEY PACKED AWAY her gear and followed Silas out of the town hall. The moon was high in the sky, giving them plenty of light to see by. It's amazing, thought Sydney, what you begin to appreciate when you have very little.

"First we start the fire and give it a chance to take hold," said Silas. "Then we topple the water tower, and then push the fire over the edge."

He stopped by a locked shed and pulled a key from his pocket. "One of my hiding places from Henry. Although he wouldn't think to take fuel, I like to keep it locked up." He grabbed two five gallon gas cans that were set just inside the door.

"Can I carry one?" she asked.

Silas shook his head. "No thanks, this keeps me balanced." He led the way to the house and handed Sydney a gas can. "Pour it over the pile here, I'll get the other side." When they had emptied the cans he shooed her out of the house.

"Stand well back. The fumes are going to explode once I set a light to them."

Sydney did as instructed. She watched Silas take something from his pocket, light it and throw it onto the pile. He turned and ran from the house.

Nothing happened. A sense of disappointment washed over Sydney. All that work for noth—a loud whoosh and a physical whump as the explosion rocked her back, followed by the crackle of flames, interrupted her thought. She retreated several feet to get away from the sudden heat.

"Holy cow! Silas are you okay?"

Silas had tripped and fallen during his mad dash away from the house. He got to his knees and shook his head, then slowly stood and looked at the burning house.

Sydney noticed a sheen of moisture covering his face. His hands trembled. After a moment she realized Silas was trembling all over.

"Is this the first fire you've been close to since Thomas tried to burn you alive?" she asked softly. She watched his Adam's apple move as he tried to speak. Finally he simply nodded his head.

Sydney took his good hand in hers and squeezed. "You're a brave man, Silas. I appreciate what you're doing to help me and Jordan. Let's go see to that water tower."

Silas gave her a grateful smile. He squeezed her fingers and dropped her hand. They turned away from the fire and jogged the few blocks to the tractor tied to the water tower. Behind them the roar of the fire grew and flames cast their flickering light onto the town.

When they reached the tractor Sydney looked from it to the tractor and frowned. "How do you plan to do this without getting pulled over the edge with the tractor?"

Silas climbed the short ladder steps into the tractor cab. He pulled a piece of two by four lumber from the floor and waved it at Sydney. "With this."

Sydney stood back, away from the tower and away from

the sinkhole. A million things could go wrong, she thought as she heard Silas start the tractor.

The rope could break. She'd gone to school with a young man who was killed by a tow chain when it snapped and whipped into his body. For sure a rope wasn't the same as a chain, but she'd read about sailors losing their legs when lines snapped and whipped across the ship's deck.

And what about the tower and water tank? What if the support column bent and twisted instead of shearing off the way Silas expected it to? What if the tank toppled onto Silas in the tractor? Or dropped sideways and broke apart?

Sydney backed away several more long steps as Silas gunned the tractor's gas pedal and slipped it into gear. The rope tightened when he moved forward until it had stretched as far as it would go. The tractor's engine whined and the rear tires spun. It wasn't powerful enough to topple the water tank.

Silas didn't quit. He rocked back and forth a few times, then kept a steady pressure on the rope again. Sydney watched the water tank begin to sway: slight movements toward the sinkhole and then back to vertical. She shouted to Silas but he couldn't hear her over the tractor engine.

A loud, harsh screech sounded from the water tank's support column. The tank swayed toward the hole and this time did not return to vertical. Sydney ran forward, shouting and waving her arms, desperate to catch Silas's attention before the tank toppled on top of him.

She saw him glance back at the tower and grin. He leaned down, did something to the tractor, and then leaped from the cab. By now the tractor was mere feet from the edge of the sinkhole. Silas rolled in the dirt and jumped to his feet. He ran toward Sydney and safety.

The tractor rumbled forward and over the edge of the

sinkhole's lip. The change in vertical dislodged the piece of wood Silas had used to hold the gas pedal down and the engine quieted. The crackle of flames replaced the roar of the tractor's engine.

The heavy rope stretched taught from the water tower down over the lip and disappeared.

Sydney chewed on her bottom lip as she watched, praying that Silas's plan would work. Nothing happened for several long moments. Then the rope snapped and the half that was tied to the support column whipped back and wrapped around the column.

Sydney turned to Silas, wondering how he would take the failure of his plan. To her surprise he merely gazed at the water tower with an expectant expression. She looked back toward the tower and saw that the water tank had fallen several degrees closer to the sinkhole. Slowly, inches at a time, the water tank continued to sag until it hovered over the hole.

Sydney's hopes flared. Silas placed a hand on her shoulder and squeezed. The unmarred side of his face held a satisfied smile. They stood that way for nearly a minute until the support column snapped with an ungodly squeal of tearing metal.

The water tank tumbled over the edge of the sinkhole and disappeared with a loud splash.

"Come on," said Silas. He turned and ran toward the fire with Sydney on his heels.

Sydney gulped when she saw how large the fire had grown. It had spread from the front room through the remainder of the house. Flames and smoke leaped high in the sky, blotting out the stars. She could feel the heat well before they reached the bulldozer. There was no way Silas could get close to the inferno with the bulldozer.

She shouted at him to forget the fire, straining to make herself heard above the fire's roar. A piece of the remaining roof collapsed into the flames adding fuel and making the impossibly high flames shoot higher.

Sydney had to admit the fire was an awe-inspiring sight. She lost track of Silas for a moment and looked around to find him. She spotted him walking toward the fire with another gas can.

What on earth does he want with that? she wondered. She gasped as he unscrewed the gas can's cap and doused himself with the contents. Silas was going to set himself on fire!

"Noooo!" she screamed. She started running toward him but Silas had already climbed into the bulldozer. The giant machine began to move forward, its tracks digging into the sunbaked ground, until the blade reached the front edge of the burning house.

Sydney tore her gaze from the sight. She couldn't bear to watch Silas burst into flames. Tears ran down her cheeks and quickly evaporated in the superheated air. She felt as though she was burning up. The heat of the fire forced her to move back.

She heard the dozer's engine straining and looked back toward the house. Silas had leaped from the machine, his clothes steaming.

Steaming? Silas should have burst into flames by now. Sydney ran forward and grabbed Silas by the arm. She dragged him, stumbling alongside her, away from the fire. The dozer continued pushing against the collapsing house until both fire and machine tumbled over the sinkhole lip.

The fire's roar receded. The air temperature dropped. Goosebumps broke out on Sydney's arms. She turned to Silas and punched his arm.

"Ow." Silas rubbed his arm and glared at her. "What was that for?"

"You scared me half to death, you-you…idiot! I thought you had poured gasoline on yourself." She choked back a sob. "I thought you were going to burst into flames right in front of me and die."

Silas's good eye blinked. He raised his only eyebrow. "You what? Why on earth would I set fire to myself? Been there, didn't like it. That was water, Sydney. I needed to soak my clothes to get close enough to set the dozer. Even with the water it was a near thing."

"Water? That was water? You could have told me, you know, instead of setting me into a panic. That was very inconsiderate of you." She dashed away her tears and wiped her nose on her sleeve.

A look of wonder came over Silas's face. "You were worried about me? Huh, imagine that. It's been a long time since anyone cared enough to worry about me." He smiled his lopsided smile. "Thank you, Sydney. I'll try not to upset you again."

Silas glanced at the light flickering from the depths of the sinkhole. "I think our little diversions should have done their job by now. It's time to go rescue your friend and his dog and the king."

Sydney opened her mouth to continue her reprimand. Common sense quickly took over. They had a mission. It was time to go.

The air in the king's chamber was stifling. Too many people, too little fresh air. Jordan tried to take shallower breaths but then he felt as if he was suffocating so he dragged in a deep breath to compensate. Mistake. The stench of dozens of unwashed bodies, all with bad breath, made him choke and gag.

He lifted his nose, searching for the slightest breath of fresh air. He detected a tiny coolness to his right and stepped in that direction.

"Where do you think you're going?" Sir Thomas sounded tense.

"I need air. I feel faint," replied Jordan.

"Air. Air," moaned the king's court.

He pushed through a couple of auras and took two more steps before Sir Thomas stopped him again. Jordan heard several people panting. He wasn't the only one suffering from the crowded quarters.

"You aren't going anywhere," said Sir Thomas. "Besides, the windows may not have any glass left in them but they're all barred. You can't escape that way."

"Well, if the windows are barred and I can't escape, what's the harm in letting me get some fresh air?" asked Jordan, making an effort to keep his temper in check. Sometimes dealing with the mentally inept was a real challenge.

"You are my prisoner. You must do as I say. Stand by the king."

Jordan reluctantly turned back and retraced the few steps to the king's side. He suspected that Sir Jordan would delight in harming someone if he didn't obey. He tilted his nose to the ceiling and tried to breath as shallowly as possible.

Apparently the atmosphere was beginning to bother Sir Thomas as well.

"I want everyone who sleeps on the lower floor to leave this room and go to bed. Two guards will go with you to make sure you obey me. Go! Now!"

Jordan watched auras race toward the door. He counted

twenty-four as they departed one by one. He breathed a heavy sigh. That should relieve some of the odor and stuffiness. But instead of spreading out as he expected them to do, the remaining auras bunched closer to him and the king.

Jordan sighed again. What could he do? These people were afraid and seeking comfort in the only way they knew how. He focused on Sir Thomas's aura and didn't care for what he saw. The colors continued to grow darker and more menacing.

Suddenly Jordan knew without a doubt that Sir Thomas planned to kill him and the king no matter what answer Sydney returned with in the morning. Sir Thomas would kill Dogma as well because the great beast would give her life to protect Jordan.

Dread chilled him. Somehow he had to find a way to save them all. The king was a nutcase, but he possessed a gentle and good soul and he didn't deserve to be tortured and murdered.

Beyond that, Jordan couldn't bear the thought of leaving Sydney to deal with Sir Thomas on her own. The thought of Sir Thomas forcing himself on Sydney made him grit his teeth in anger. There was no way he'd ever let that happen.

Sir Thomas's aura moved toward the door. "Get in here and watch the prisoners," he said. Two auras entered the room and stood beside the door. "I'll be back shortly. I'm going to check on the others. Kill anyone who tries to escape."

This was his chance. Unfortunately Jordan was out of great ideas. Sydney had told him that Sir Thomas had taken his staff from the king. The staff was the only weapon he knew how to wield.

He looked at the confusion of auras huddled next to him.

The other prisoners would be of no help. He searched the auras for Angeline and found her crouched next to the king.

"Angeline." Jordan whispered her name so softly he could barely hear it himself.

Angeline's aura stood and moved closer to him. "We have to save the king," she whispered. "We can't let him die."

"I know. But I don't have a plan. Do you have any ideas?"

"I could try to distract the guards by offering them my body. That's the only thing I can think of to do."

Jordan shook his head. "No. I'm sure they'd go for it but then what? I didn't mention this before because it didn't seem important at the time, but I'm blind, Angeline. I know where people are because I can see their auras, but I can't see what they're doing."

"Blind? But you can't be, you get around so well."

Jordan scowled. "I get around, but I'm definitely blind. We need a man who can see to help us. Can you find someone from this group we can trust?"

"No," said Angeline firmly. "Everyone here now is from the third floor, the more disturbed or difficult patients. There might have been someone from the group Sir Thomas sent to bed, most of them can function fairly well. But this group? Only the king could help, and he's tied up and gagged."

"Then we need a big diversion. What about the fire? Sir Thomas is a firebug. What if we throw all the wood on the fire at once?"

"Are you stupid?" asked Angeline. "That's a horrible idea. Sir Thomas will just toss a few of us onto the flames."

Jordan was about to argue with her when he saw Sir Thomas's aura return. "Too late," he muttered. Damn it, time was running out. He had to do something.

Off in the distance, but not that far away, he realized, he

heard a roar, then the screech of tearing metal. The sound reminded him of the accident that cost his parent's lives and his sight. He shuddered. The king's court moaned and whimpered.

Jordan heard a splash and the roaring stopped. A few seconds later a great crash shook the building.

"What the hell was that?" asked Sir Thomas.

"How are we supposed to know?" replied Jordan. "We're stuck in here with you. Maybe the light hole collapsed again. Perhaps you'd better check. It would be a shame to take over a doomed kingdom."

"Doooom, doooom," moaned the king's court.

Jordan shook his head. If their situation wasn't quite so dire the king's court would be quite entertaining. He watched Sir Thomas's aura flare and knew the bastard was worried. Good. If they were lucky this diversion would create an opportunity for them to escape.

"Sir Michael, go see what's going on out there. Report back to me as fast as you can." Sir Thomas's voice sounded strained.

One of the guards left the king's chamber. Less than a minute later a half dozen auras came rushing into the room.

"We're doomed!" they cried.

"Doomed! Doomed!" echoed the court, louder and more panicked now.

"Shut up, you morons," snarled Sir Thomas. "We aren't doomed. We're safe, there's no earth over Graceville to fall down on us. The crash sounded near the lip to the right. I'm sure it's just the light hole expanding. Go back to bed. I don't need you here adding to the chaos."

The newcomers ignored Sir Thomas. They joined the group huddled around Jordan and the king, muttering and moaning about the end of the world.

Jordan felt a moment of pity and sympathy. The changes wrought by the earth's upheaval had overwhelmed the people who possessed all their faculties. It must have been terrifying for the patients here at Graceville.

The guard returned and whispered something to Sir Thomas.

"What is it, Sir Michael?" asked Jordan. "The patients are concerned. We all want to know what made that loud crash."

"The water tower from the town overhead collapsed into the lake," answered Sir Thomas. "Nothing to worry about." His voice became harder and colder. "As for you, Sir Jordan, your wife has three hours left. If she hasn't returned by then you die. I suggest you worry about that instead."

Another roar, this one infinitely more terrifying than the last, tore through the air. The patients pressed closer to Jordan, so close that he couldn't even lift his arms. Dogma growled and the pressure eased.

The sound of crackling flames reached them, followed a moment later by the smell of fire. Within moments the room seemed to fill with smoke.

"On the floor everyone," commanded Jordan. He dropped to his hands and knees and prayed everyone would imitate him. The smoke would rise. The safest place to be was near the floor.

Angeline grabbed his arm. "The king! We have to get him down here with us," she said.

"Where is Sir Thomas, can you see him?" He waited impatiently for Angeline's answer.

"No. I think he left. Help me untie the king." Angeline stood and tugged on Jordan's arm.

Jordan reached toward the king's aura until he felt flesh and muscle. "Sorry, your majesty," he said as he patted the king's body. "I don't mean to offend you." Jordan realized he was patting the king's leg.

He followed a shin to a knee and on up the leg until he found ropes securing the king's thighs to the chair. He ran his fingers over the ropes and found a massive knot on the side of the chair.

"Oh brother. What I wouldn't give for a knife right now." Jordan struggled with the knot. Untying knots was not something he had ever practiced. Given enough time he felt sure he'd get it, but time was not a luxury he had right now. He made a frustrated growl in his throat.

"Steadfast, Loyal, and True."

Jordan looked up. Angeline must have removed the king's gag. A piercing desire to see the face that went with that sonorous voice went through him. He pushed it aside and forced his attention back to the knot. He had learned long ago not to dwell on 'what-ifs' and 'if-onlys'—they only led to dissatisfaction with life.

The smoke grew thicker, the smell of burning wood and chemicals and fuel permeating the king's chamber. Jordan concentrated on the tangled knot and tried to ignore his rising panic.

"Nice to hear your voice again, Your Highness," Jordan said, striving for a conversational tone. Speaking as if all was normal helped calm him. "I'm doing my best here, but knots are not my specialty. I have to admit I'm getting a little frustrated."

"How Do You Think I Feel?" replied the king.

Jordan shook his head in wonder. It really was quite amazing how the king managed to speak in only song titles and get his point across. Only Elvis song titles, he corrected. Even more impressive.

"I don't know how you do it sir, but I am amazed by your

abilities," he said aloud. "You are quite the cat's ass, as my dear sister used to say."

"Cat's assss, cat's assss," hissed the others, sounding like a room full of deflating balloons.

The knot loosened under Jordan's fingers and he almost shouted with relief. The secret to untying a knot is to break its back. He would remember that.

"All right, your majesty, we're making progress. One down. Excuse me while I touch you again to look for the other knot."

Jordan ran his hands lightly over the king's thighs, recalling Sydney's comment about the king being built like a sumo wrestler. She hadn't exaggerated.

His fingers finally found the second knot and he went to work on it. Now that he knew the secret, it came apart much faster than the first one had.

"Catchin' On Fast," said the king. He rolled out of the chair and joined the others on the floor. "Only The Strong Survive."

Silas stopped by his shed on their way back to the access hole. He grabbed a coil of climbing rope and a gold-topped cane, then relocked the shed door and pocketed the key.

Sydney left her pack in the town hall. She carried her knife and the useless bolts for her crossbow in hopes she would get it back. They hurried on to the stump and rope ladder and were soon descending the cliff stairs into Graceville.

"What's the cane for?" asked Sydney when they reached the bottom step.

Silas handed her the cane to give her a better look at it.

It was heavier than she expected. The bottom was tipped with a brass thimble, the top capped with a shiny brass eagle. The shaft appeared to be ebony wood. It was obviously an heirloom quality, expensive cane.

Silas took it back and grasped the shaft and head firmly. He pulled it apart, revealing a long, thin dagger.

"This belonged to my father," he said as he reseated the dagger with a firm snap.

"Thomas coveted this cane. I think if he'd been allowed to

go on as he was he would've eventually killed my father to possess it."

Sydney recognized the predatory gleam that came into his eye. Silas had been an ordinary man at one time but the fire had changed him. He possessed a dangerous edge now that people would be wise to heed.

They wasted no time descending the rope ladder. Soon they stood on Graceville's main street. This end of town was quiet and mostly dark but for the glow from the fire burning at the opposite end of town. The flames cast enough light for them to see their footing and they moved quickly to the center of town.

Sydney heard voices shouting and saw several shadows running back and forth in front of the fire. She turned toward Silas and spoke low into his good ear. Even though they were still a fair distance from the fire she didn't want to risk alerting Thomas of their presence.

"You said you've been here before, Silas?" she asked.

"Once," he replied. "I came to check on the king. Elvis and I were friends as teenagers, before Thomas wreaked havoc with our lives. I stayed long enough to be sure the king survived the fall into the aquifer and then left. He never knew I was here."

Sydney looked at Silas in surprise. "The king's real name is Elvis? I don't believe it."

Silas chuckled. "I know, quite the coincidence, isn't it? Actually I think Elvis became a Presley fan at first because they shared a name. Then he grew to love Presley's music. And of course he, the king I mean, was always meant to sing. Have you heard his voice?"

Sydney assured him she had not only spoken with the king, but she had heard him sing and he was indeed magical.

"We were told that he overdosed at an Elvis Presley concert," she said. "Do you know if that's true?"

A hard look came over Silas's face. "Yeah, it's true, but it wasn't the king's doing. A couple badasses from school snuck too many hits of LSD into his pop. Elvis was a teetotaler and wouldn't touch drugs. He had a dream—he wanted to be a professional singer—and he didn't waste his time doing drugs or drinking like many of the other kids we went to school with."

"That's horrible," said Sydney. "How could anyone do such a thing? I can't imagine how awful it must have been for him. He must have thought he was truly going crazy."

Silas shrugged his good shoulder. "He did go crazy, Sydney. For a long time he didn't know what was real and what he was hallucinating. He couldn't function anymore without someone looking after him."

"Did you find the kids who drugged him?"

"Oh yeah."

Sydney had a terrible premonition. "Don't tell me. Was Thomas one of them? And does the king know?"

"Good guess. Yes, Thomas drugged my best friend and turned him into a fruitcake. And no, I never told Elvis. It wouldn't have helped. Now it's just one more reason for me to take my revenge."

They reached the center of town and carefully worked their way through the piles of rubble and entered the asylum. Once inside they stopped in silent accord and listened. The heavy door blocked the shouts from outside. The windowless stairwell was quiet and dark, a haven from the chaos going on around them.

Sydney moved forward and began to climb the stairs with Silas close on her heels. They stopped at the first floor and opened the door and again listened. Sydney heard frightened muttering coming from several rooms. The smell of smoke permeated the hallway.

"I need to check on someone," she said, and entered the hall. She stopped at the fifth door on the right and poked her head around the door opening.

"Sir Lewie? Are you in here?"

The windows on this side of the building were faintly lit by the fire. She saw a shadow detach itself from the far corner and take a hesitant step toward her.

"Ghost of Christmas Future, is that you? Have you brought me my cannon? Now would be a good time, you know. The earth is falling apart again and I need to get away from here." Sir Lewis and Clark's thin, reedy voice cracked with fear.

Sydney crossed the room and stood next to the man she'd never seen. She placed her hand on his arm. He flinched, then stood trembling next to her.

"Yes, it's me, the Ghost of Christmas Future," she said, giving his arm a light pat. "I stopped by to tell you that there's nothing to worry about. The earth is not falling apart again. My, uh, partner and I are trying to rescue the king and Sir Jordan from Sir Thomas."

"Sir Thomas plans to kill the king and Sir Jordan. He has commanded us all to watch." Sir Lewis and Clark shook his head repeatedly. "I cannot. I cannot. I cannot watch. It is wrong to kill the king." His voice rose in pitch.

Sydney stroked his arm. The man's distress was painful to witness and made her heart ache. How awful it must be for these people. They have such little control over themselves or their lives.

"Shhh," she crooned, still stroking Sir Lewis and Clark's arm. "You will not have to watch Sir Thomas kill the king, Sir Lewie. I, the Ghost of Christmas Future, make you that promise. Is Sir Thomas still holding everyone in the king's chamber?"

Sir Lewis and Clark calmed. "No. He sent everyone on this floor to our rooms but many stayed with the king. I wonder when you intend to bring me my cannon. I am wasting time here when I could be exploring the far side of the great lake."

Sydney smiled. Some of the people living in the asylum reminded her of children. Easily mollified, easily distracted, and yet sometimes completely focused on their objective, whether it be finagling a different color lipstick or acquiring a cannon.

She gave Sir Lewis and Clark's arm a final pat and headed toward the door. "I will see about your cannon after I deal with Sir Thomas," she promised.

She found Silas waiting for her outside the room. "A cannon? Is he serious?" he whispered.

"Apparently so," answered Sydney. "I wanted to make sure he was okay, and see if he knew anything helpful, although I suppose it's next to impossible to get useful information from most of the patients."

"You're a good person, Sydney Waters," said Silas. "Where to next?"

"If only you knew," muttered Sydney under breath. She was not a good person. But Silas would never know that because she would never tell him the truth about her past.

"Upstairs to the king's chamber," she said aloud. She led the way to the rear hallway door and up the next flight of stairs. Without the light from the burning house, the halls and stairwells were velvety dark.

The smoke seemed worse on the top floor. If it grew any thicker they'd have to evacuate everyone from the building.

She wondered if evacuation was even possible. Some of these people never left the asylum.

Sydney carefully made her way along the corridor to the king's chamber with Silas close on her heels. The smoke continued to thicken and obscure most of the light cast by the flames. She saw no sign of the guards Sir Thomas had left outside the door.

She stopped outside the king's room and wondered what to do next. She heard the rumble of the king's voice. When she had fled this room he had been gagged. What did it mean? Had they overcome Sir Thomas and freed the king?

She heard the king say, "Only The Strong Survive," and Silas slipped past her and through the door.

"You got that right, Elvis," said Silas. "Long time no see. How are you old boy?"

Jordan lifted his head and looked toward the new voice. A clear, bright, asymmetrical aura advanced upon them. Another aura appeared behind it and he let out the breath he hadn't realized he was holding. Sydney had returned.

"Hey. Hey. Hey. I Don't Wanna Be Tied," said the king.

"Looks like someone already took care of that, Elvis," replied Silas, noting the ropes on the floor. "You're looking good. Is that snake Sir Thomas around here somewhere?"

Sydney made her way to Jordan and dropped to her hands and knees. She looked him over in the flickering light and didn't see any new wounds. Thomas hadn't hurt him— yet. Some of the tension drained from her body.

"You all right?" she whispered into his ear.

"Yes, Sir Thomas was waiting to torture us. I think he wanted you here to observe his technique or something equally as twisted. What's the smoke from? Did you set the town on fire?"

Sydney's soft breath tickled his ear. He fought the urge to

turn his head and kiss her. Now was not the time. They had to deal with Sir Thomas before the man hurt somebody.

"We set a house on fire and pushed it over the rim of the sinkhole," replied Sydney. Dogma nuzzled her neck and she hugged the great beast. "I'm happy to see you too, beautiful. You did good watching over our friend."

She turned her attention back to Jordan. "Silas pushed the town's water tower into the sinkhole too. We were hoping to create a diversion."

"Silas?" Jordan frowned. Who the devil was Silas?

"I'll tell you everything later. Right now we need to get everyone to the other side of the building where the smoke isn't as bad."

Sydney stood and called for everyone's attention. "We have to leave the king's chamber until the fire burns out," she told them. "The air is better on the other side of the building so I want us all to move to a room off the other hallway."

"Flaming Star," said the king.

"Not a star exactly, Your Highness," said Silas. "More like a flaming house. What was left of the mayor's house, to be precise. He won't miss it, he's long gone. Let me help you into your throne and I'll wheel you to another room. You and your court can wait there until we can take care of Sir Thomas."

It took a great deal of huffing and puffing, but with Sydney and Angeline's help Silas eventually managed to get the king back on his throne. He quickly wheeled him from the room with the king's court following close behind.

Sydney led them to the room she and Jordan had slept in earlier.

"Now what," she asked Silas after they had everyone semi-settled.

"We have to find Thomas," he replied. "He cannot be

allowed to remain here. If we leave him it will only be a matter of time until he pulls this again. Elvis won't be safe as long as Thomas is alive."

Dread filled Sydney. She had hoped to deal with the problem of Sir Thomas without taking any lives. She took a deep, shuddering breath and let it out. Then another. She looked at the scarred half of Silas's face and neck and knew what had to be done.

Someone had to stand against evil.

Accept your fate, Sydney, she told herself resignedly. The people of Graceville were defenseless and could not take care of themselves. They needed to be protected from Thomas's twisted mind.

She and Silas were the only ones there who could deal with the problem.

"I agree," she said aloud. "We need to find Sir Thomas."

Silas walked over to Jordan and extended his hand. When Jordan didn't respond he hastily dropped it.

"My apologies, Mr. James. You do not behave like a blind man and it is easy to forget that you cannot see. My name is Silas Goodyear. I'm very pleased to make your acquaintance. Sydney speaks highly of you."

"You have me at a disadvantage Mr. Goodyear. I know nothing about you," said Jordan. He knew he sounded like a jerk but he couldn't help it. He felt jealous of Silas's obvious friendship with Sydney.

"I hope we have the opportunity to become friends when this is over, Jordan. I have admired your work and followed your career with great interest. Before Thomas tried to burn me alive, Elvis and I had a band. We were just young teens fooling around, but with the king's talent we might have been mildly successful. Believe it or not I had a decent voice then myself."

Jordan didn't know what to say. Thomas had set this man on fire? Understanding suddenly flashed. Silas had to be the "adopted" brother Thomas had mentioned. The one he hated.

Perhaps being burned explained Silas's oddly shaped aura. He suppressed a shudder at the thought and then felt ashamed. He wished he hadn't just acted like an ass.

"I promise to keep a close eye on Sydney and keep her safe," continued Silas. "She's a beautiful girl with a kind soul and a great deal of courage, and it's obvious you two care for one another. I promise I won't let Thomas hurt her."

Jordan watched the strangely asymmetrical aura walk away. Other than its shape, Silas's aura looked healthy, although his voice sounded creepy. He hoped he could trust the guy.

He wondered where Sydney had found Silas. He tried to shake how he felt seeing their auras leave together. It was an ugly feeling; envy and possessiveness wrapped up with a little fear. I'm jealous, he finally realized with surprise. He didn't care for the emotion, it made him feel weak and small.

Jordan turned toward the king. "Are you doing okay, your majesty?" He wished he could ask the king about Silas. Somehow he didn't think song titles would tell him what he wanted to know.

"Doin' the Best I Can," came the reply.

"Doin' the can-can," echoed the court.

Jordan smiled. Ignorance was truly bliss.

Sydney followed Silas through the rubble outside the asylum. She had located the man with her crossbow pistol and persuaded him to return it to her in exchange for a can of peanut butter, to be delivered after the crisis was over. He had been reluctant to trust her, but she had reminded him that she was a princess, and princesses did not lie.

The loaded crossbow boosted her confidence. She knew she couldn't win in a hand-to-hand fight against Thomas or one of his minions, but the crossbow gave her the advantage of being able to attack from a short distance. It was no good for a long shot, but it was better than no weapon at all.

The smoke from the fire filled the spaces around Graceville, a thick unmoving blanket that burned Sydney's eyes and throat.

Silas handed her a wet bandana. "Tie this around your nose and mouth," he said. "It won't protect your eyes but it will help you breath. The good news is that the smoke will give us some cover while we look for Thomas."

Sydney didn't waste her breath asking him where he got the bandanas. Silas had proved to be a very resourceful guy. She tied the bandana onto her face and immediately breathed a little easier. Silas grabbed her hand, pulled her into a narrow alley between two shanties, and they headed toward the lake.

The alley was mostly clear of smoke and she blinked her eyes in relief. Unfortunately the relief was short-lived. When they reached the farther edge of the buildings they plunged back into the thick haze.

Sydney squinted until her eyes were almost shut. It helped the burning, but not as much as she would've liked. She was glad Silas still held her hand and led the way.

They slowly made their way along the lake edge toward the still-burning house. Their bodies created the only air movement, dragging the motionless smoke behind them and creating swirling smoke devils, mini tornadoes that lasted for mere seconds before winking out.

Sydney caught a glimpse through the smoke of a hulking

shape off to her left. She stopped and tugged on Silas's hand.

"What's that?" she asked and pointed. They stood and stared at the shape for a few moments, until Silas gave a raspy chuckle.

"It's the water tower," he said. "It's half submerged in the lake. The support column snapped off. It looks a little like a fat, surfaced submarine, doesn't it?"

Sydney stared at the water tower for another minute. It did look like a surfaced submarine. The remaining stub of the support column looked like the sub's hatch.

An idea began to take shape in the back of her mind. Before she could clarify it Silas headed toward the burning house again and she hustled to catch up with him.

Silas's steps slowed as they drew closer to the fire. Sydney noticed his clenched jaw and placed her hand on his arm to stop him.

"Are you okay, Silas? We don't have to get any closer. I'm sure we can set up an ambush for Thomas and catch him on his way back to the asylum."

Silas shook his head. "No. I admit being this close to fire is a bit nerve-wracking, but I'll be fine. We need to find Thomas before he hurts someone."

They had only moved a few steps closer when they heard shouting coming from the right side of the burning house, opposite the lake. Silas grabbed Sydney's hand again and pulled her between the last pair of shanties.

They reached the street and cautiously looked around the corner of the small shanty. Two men stood fifty feet away, backlit by the flames as they stood watching the fire. The fire had burnt down and no longer cast as much light. A loud pop sent a jet of sparks shooting skyward and the men jumped and shouted with glee.

"Now what?" asked Sydney. "I can't tell if one of those

men is Thomas. We need to get closer, but there's no cover. He had three guards, so two people are missing. Maybe they're on the other side of the fire I suppose."

"You wait here," rasped Silas. "I'll get as close as I can and see if one of them is Thomas."

Silas took two steps into the open. An explosion rocked the ground and blew the two men and Silas backward. Sparks and chunks of burning house rained down on them.

Sydney heard a rumble overhead and looked up in time to see a chunk of earth fall next to the burning house. The explosion had knocked the edge of the sinkhole loose.

She saw a black shape hanging over the sinkhole lip and realized a building hung there unsupported. A loud crack sounded overhead. She watched in awe as the building tumbled down and collapsed next to the fire. Within moments it too was in flames.

"Silas! Are you okay?" Sydney darted out from her hiding place and grabbed Silas by the arm. She helped him to his feet and led him back behind the shanty, out of sight of Thomas's men.

The shockwave from the explosion had dispersed most of the heavy cloud of gray smoke. In its place rose a black plume.

"What exploded? Do you know?" asked Sydney. She had to shout to be heard over the roar of the renewed fire.

"I think it was the fuel tank from the dozer. It must have cracked when it fell into the sinkhole. I never considered that possibility." He looked at the fire and frowned. "I don't see those two men anymore. I wonder where they went."

Something crackled overhead. Sydney looked up and realized the roof of the shanty they were hiding behind was in flames. She grabbed at Silas and pulled him into the street.

"Silas! We have to get back to the asylum. These shanties

are all built of wood. They're going to catch fire and burn and we have no way to stop it. We have to evacuate the patients and move them somewhere safe until this burns out. Come on."

Sydney didn't wait to see if Silas was following her. She had to get to Jordan and there was no time to waste. She ran down the street to the asylum and quickly made her way through the rubble path. The newly enlarged fire burned nearly as bright as daylight and made it easy to make her way without tripping.

She flung open the door and stepped inside. A hand grabbed her wrist and pulled her off balance.

"I've been waiting for you, Princess," said Sir Thomas in her ear. He slipped the crossbow from her shoulder and twisted her arm behind her back.

"Up the stairs. It's time to deal with your husband and get rid of the king. I'm sure they're eagerly awaiting my return."

He chuckled, a laugh low and ominous that held no trace of humor.

Sydney started up the stairs, propelled by Sir Thomas. She tried to wriggle free but he only pushed her hand higher. Her shoulder screamed in protest. She fought down the panic that threatened to overwhelm her. Silas is somewhere behind us, she reminded herself. Surely he'd free her from Sir Thomas.

"How the hell did a little girl like you come up with the idea for the burning house? That was a stroke of genius. I know you're clever, but something tells me you had help. I wonder who that was…"

Sydney could almost hear the wheels turning in Sir Thomas's mind. She had to keep Silas's presence a secret; he would need the element of surprise to overcome Thomas.

"I found the dozer in one of the barns. It had a little fuel left. No one thought to check it before they abandoned the town I guess." Sydney cleared her throat. She tried to keep her tone light and conversational, as if being held captive by a madman was nothing out of the ordinary.

"Anyway," she continued, "it gave me an idea. Jordan told me you were partial to fires. I thought maybe I could distract you and sneak Jordan out of here."

They reached the first landing. Sir Thomas jerked her to a stop. "Then why were you sneaking around town, and who was that with you? I saw you peeking around Angeline's shanty, so don't lie to me." His voice was suddenly low and menacing in Sydney's ear. "I hate liars."

She shuddered. "I'm not lying. I was sneaking around town, as you call it, to find out where you were. I didn't want to risk running into you with Jordan." She turned to start up the next flight of stairs but Sir Thomas yanked her back. This time she couldn't suppress a gasp of pain.

"You still haven't answered my question," he said, angry now. "Who were you with? I clearly saw a man with you."

"That was Sir Lewis and Clark," she replied, silently apologizing to the harmless explorer for bringing up his name. "He thinks I'm the Ghost of Christmas Future. I talked him into coming with me but the fire scared him and he ran back here."

They stood on the landing for what felt like an eternity while her captor considered her story. Sydney relaxed a little when he directed her to continue up the stairs. They skipped the second floor and made their way to the third.

"Open the door," commanded Sir Thomas.

Sydney reached forward with her free hand and pulled the door open. A thick cloud of smoke blew into the stairwell and choked her. Coughing, eyes watering, she let the door fall shut again.

"We can't go in there," she said. She waited for another coughing fit to pass. "We'll suffocate in that smoke. If the king and Jordan and the king's followers are in his chambers they must be unconscious, or even dead, by now." She hoped those words were another lie, hoped that somehow Jordan had taken everyone to a safer place.

Sir Thomas swore. Sydney felt his growing anger and frustration. His plan was not going as he expected. She sent a prayer of thanks to Silas for his diversions and wondered where he was.

"The smoke is all on this side of the building," said Sir Thomas. "If your Jordan has any brains he would've moved everyone to the opposite side. That's what I'd do if I was in his shoes. We'll check the other hallway."

"What about your guards? Aren't they watching the king and Jordan? And how will we get to the other hallway?" asked Sydney. "Is there another entrance on the other side of the building?"

Sir Thomas tugged her around and pushed her down the stairs without answering. With him behind and above her, the pressure on her shoulder was fast becoming unbearable. Anger began to replace Sydney's fear. She hated being manhandled.

There was no call for physical abuse, her mother always said, and Sydney agreed. She had suffered her one and only spanking when she was about five after she'd put her small fist through the back door window in an angry snit.

She'd never forgotten the shock and humiliation of being struck, even if she had deserved it. Nor would she ever forget the tears in her father's eyes and the way his hand trembled when he'd spanked her. He'd hugged her tight afterward and told her the spanking hurt him as much as it did her.

She didn't believe him at the time but now that she was

older she saw that spanking had not been not part of her father's make-up. He had been a peaceful man through and through. Unlike the scary creep that held her captive now.

"Sir Thomas, do you think you could ease up a bit on my shoulder? I'm afraid you're going to dislocate it. Besides, you have no right to take me prisoner. You set me free and agreed to give me until morning to decide what to do. It's still night-time, so technically you are reneging on your deal. That's not very chivalrous of you."

Sir Thomas stopped and Sydney cried out as she continued down a step and her arm was jerked higher. She quickly stumbled back to the step above. The pain in her shoulder made her pant.

"That was before you set fire to the town," said Thomas. "All deals are off now. But I will let your arm go because I need both of my hands free."

He released Sydney's arm. A fresh wave of pain almost dropped her but she forced her knees to lock as she gently rubbed her shoulder.

"Put both your hands behind you." Thomas didn't wait for her to comply. He grabbed Sydney's elbows and pulled her arms back.

A moment later she felt a plastic zip tie tighten around her wrists. She struggled against it but the tie cut into her skin and held her wrists firm. This was far worse than having one arm held behind her back. She was completely helpless now.

"Just one of the many useful items that Sir Henry found on one of his scrounging trips. I knew I'd need it eventually, although I always thought I'd be using it on the king."

Sir Thomas sounded positively cheerful. He grabbed Sydney by an elbow and led her down the steps and out of the building.

She was shocked to see that the fire had spread through the half the town. All the wooden structures to the right of the asylum were ablaze. The roar and heat from the fire was almost unbearable. Still no sign of Silas.

She wondered if being so close to the flames had proven too much for Silas to face. She couldn't blame him after what Sir Thomas had done to him, but she prayed that he hadn't abandoned her. She desperately needed his help.

Sydney stumbled after Sir Thomas through the rubbled path. She glanced back at the brick building and saw that the yellow brick was now streaked with black. She prayed that the inmates who slept on that side of the hospital had sense enough to evacuate their rooms. She didn't want to add the guilt of their deaths to the burden she already carried.

She bumped against Sir Thomas and realized he had stopped. He stood facing the fire, slack-jawed and wide-eyed, a blend of rapt wonder and excitement in his eyes. His expression reminded her of a neighbor back home, a well-respected volunteer fireman for their small town, named Mark Kline.

Mark Kline never missed a fire. Sydney had seen that expression on Mr. Kline's face once while the fire squad contained a barn fire. Two years and half a dozen high profile fires later they discovered that Mark Kline was an arsonist. He had set many of the same fires he had fought.

Sir Thomas's love and fascination for fire was not uncommon, but it was his inability to control and channel this fascination in a positive way that made him a monster.

As if reading her thoughts he turned to look at Sydney and smiled. "I think it's time to get Jordan and the king. I feel like a roast."

THE KING'S subjects were wild with panic. Their auras bounced and slammed into one another, reminding Jordan of the Mexican jumping beans his sister had sent him for his sixth birthday. The beans had hopped in the palm of his hand, enthralling him until he learned they were not beans at all, but a seedpod containing the larvae of a small moth.

Jordan tried to reassure them but he was having trouble being heard above their babble and the roar of the fire. He reached out to feel for the king's large shoulder and leaned down to speak in his ear.

"I think perhaps we should persuade your subjects to evacuate the building, Your Highness."

"Such An Easy Question. Find Out What's Happening," answered the king.

"Um, I know what's happening, Your Highness. The town is on fire. It's no longer safe here." He watched Angeline/Bethany's aura approach and stop on the opposite side of the king.

"The hospital is built from brick and cement, Sir Jordan. We're safer here than anywhere else," she said. "Besides, many of these people haven't left the building in years. I don't know if they're capable of handling the trauma of going outside."

"The roof isn't brick or cement, Beth—Angeline." Jordan remembered to call her Angeline at the last moment. He cleared his throat, hoped the king had missed his gaff.

"The roof is flammable. If any stray sparks land up there it's going to burn. We should at least move everyone to the next floor down. That way, if the roof catches fire and collapses we'll be protected by this floor."

Angeline placed her hand on the king's arm. "Sir Jordan is right, your majesty. We would all be safer downstairs. They'll follow you. Can you walk?"

"I Slipped, I Stumbled, I Fell," answered the king.

"You fell the last time you tried to walk?" asked Jordan. He couldn't lift the king by himself. He wondered if any of the king's followers were coherent enough to help.

"I Just Can't Make It By Myself. I Need Someone To Lean On," replied the king.

"We can work with that," said Angeline. "Jordan is quite tall and strong. He can support you and we'll ask Sir William to help on your other side. I'll take the throne down ahead of you and have it waiting."

"Sound Advice. Sweet Angeline. Steadfast, Loyal, and True."

"That's me your majesty," said Angeline. "Loyal and true. Do you think you can get everyone to come with us?"

"C'mon Everybody. We're Gonna Move," bellowed the king.

Silence. Sir William wormed his way through the group and stood in front of the king.

"Sir William of the green knights reporting for duty, your majesty. Where are we going?"

"Down In The Alley. In The Garden." The king's voice sounded firm and decisive.

Jordan looked at him in surprise. "You want to leave the building, Your Highness? Are you sure?"

"It's Now Or Never. I've Got Confidence. Lead Me, Guide Me. I'm Counting On You."

"Lead us, guide us," chanted the king's followers.

Jordan took a deep breath and let it out. Who was he to deny the king? "Angeline, can you push the king to the rear staircase? Sir William, where are you? Do you think you could help me get the king on his feet? Where's Sir Henry?"

The blue knight pushed his way forward. "Here, Sir Jordan. What can I do?"

"I want you to take the king's throne and carry it down the back stairs after we get him on his feet. Wait for us at the bottom of the stairs."

Everyone followed Angeline out of the room to the rear stairs.

"Sir William, where are you?" asked Jordan. He couldn't tell the knight's aura apart from the others that crowded around them.

"Right beside you, Sir Jordan."

"Sorry, I didn't see you in the crowd." The last thing Jordan wanted right now was for the king's followers to lose faith in him. If they discovered that he was blind they wouldn't trust him enough to lead them to safety. He said a silent prayer that he was indeed worthy of their trust.

Jordan tried to wrap a hand around the king's bicep and realized it was too big for him to get a firm grip. He place one hand under the king's elbow instead and the other under his armpit. Sir William's aura moved to the king's other side.

Jordan hoped the knight had a strong grip. Unfortunately

auras didn't tell him body shape or build. Sir William could be the proverbial ninety pound weakling for all he knew.

"Ready? On the count of three we pull the king onto his feet. One."

"Wait. Do we pull when you say three or after you say three?" asked Sir William.

Jordan heard the panic in the knight's voice and reminded himself that he needed to be patient and very, very clear with these people.

"On three, not after." "Ready? One, two, three!" He grunted with the effort of lifting an extremely awkward and heavy object. "Help us out here, king. Push up. On your feet. Up!"

"Up, up, UP," chanted the king's court.

The king rose several inches as if levitated by the chanting, then sagged back toward the chair.

Jordan gritted his teeth. "No you don't, Your Highness. Stand up! Up!" He felt the king engage his legs and push.

"Ohhhh, the king is up! The king is up!" shouted the king's court as his majesty gained his feet. They began to dance and gyrate in the hall.

Jordan felt the king trembling under his hands. "Good job, Your Highness, that was the hardest part. It's all downhill from here and then we'll get you back onto your throne."

"Doin The Best I Can," huffed the king. He shuffled a foot forward. With both Jordan and Sir William supporting him he made his way through the door to the stairs.

Jordan shifted his grip on the king, looking for better leverage. He was no weakling, his sister had made sure of that, incorporating a weight training program into his daily schedule. Even so, he struggled to hold the king upright. The man was incredibly large and heavy. If he wasn't such a gentle creature he'd be formidable, thought Jordan with a grunt.

"Let's rest here a moment, your majesty," said Angeline from behind them. "We don't want to overdo it and give you a heart attack."

"Wheels On My Heels, I Need You So," said the king.

Jordan chuckled. "That would be useful, wouldn't it?"

He turned toward the auras crowded around him. "Would some of you go down the stairs ahead of the king, please?" He didn't tell them that he wanted something to break the king's fall if he and Sir William should lose their hold on their fleshy ruler.

The entire court surged forward and jostled by Jordan. He planted his feet and held firm as he realized he should have picked people to go down the steps first. Ah heck, what did it matter? This way there would be plenty of bodies to stop the king if he fell, with the added bonus of knowing everyone was safely out of the building.

They waited for the last stragglers to start down the stairs, then shuffled forward to the first step and stopped. No matter how they tried they couldn't work out a way to hold the king upright while descending the stairs. If Sir William and Jordan stepped down first the king lost his support. If they tried to lower the king first they'd lose their hold on him.

Just when Jordan was beginning to believe they were stuck in the building after all, Angeline came to their rescue.

"Set him down. He can scoot down the steps on his bottom, just like a toddler would. That way he can descend under his own power and he can't fall and get hurt."

"Angeline, that's brilliant," said Jordan with heartfelt relief. He and Sir William lowered the king to the top step.

"I'll descend in front of you, Your Highness, just in case you need me," said Jordan.

He walked down a couple steps and waited for the king to reach him, then descended a few more. Angeline and Sir William followed behind the king. Step by slow, painful step they descended, letting the king rest after every couple of steps.

Jordan knew they were taking too long but there was nothing he could do about it. He took a deep breath and picked up the odor of smoke. That wasn't good. He wondered if they were going to escape the building only to find themselves in a thick cloud of unbreathable air. What choice did they have? They would be safer outside.

He wished he knew where Sydney had gotten off to. Was she still with Silas? And where was Sir Thomas? Had he set the rest of the town afire? What if he was waiting to ambush Jordan and the king when they exited the building? Sometimes being blind was more than he could bear.

———

A heavy blanket of thick smoke hung over the town. The initial roar of the fire had quieted some. It hadn't taken long for the flames to consume the shanties to the right of the brick asylum. Most had collapsed in on themselves, reduced to glowing piles of superheated coals.

Sydney glanced through a break in the smoke and saw a pale gray light filling the light hole. Dawn was fast approaching. Time was running out for Jordan and the king. She tested the tie holding her wrists together, but only succeeded in digging it deeper into her flesh.

"Walk faster," demanded Sir Thomas as he pulled on her arm.

Sydney stumbled and swore. She tried to jerk her arm free but Sir Thomas kept an iron grip on her bicep. She gritted her teeth against the pain and struggled to keep pace with Sir Thomas's hurried stride.

"What's the rush?" she asked. "It's not as if Jordan and the king have anywhere to go. You know they'll be waiting for you."

Sir Thomas whipped his head around and leered at Sydney. He lowered his mouth to her ear. "Maybe I'm eager to claim you as my bride," he said and licked her ear.

"Ew! That's disgusting." Sydney shuddered and tried to wipe her ear on her shoulder, not an easy task with her hands tied behind her back.

She glared at Sir Thomas. "Even if you succeed in getting rid of Jordan and the king,"–she refused to use the word kill–"I will never consent to marry you."

Sir Thomas didn't bother to reply. They reached the asylum and he led the way through the rubble path and into the building.

The smoke lay thick in the stairwell. Sydney choked, coughed, and forced herself to breath shallowly through her mouth. Sir Thomas led her up the stairs to the top floor and down the hall to the king's chamber. He uttered a long litany of cuss words and slammed Jordan's staff against the wall when he saw the empty room.

"Where are they?" he shouted.

He glared at Sydney who merely shrugged and pressed her lips together to hide her smile. Somehow Jordan had gotten the king to leave his chambers. What an amazing feat.

Sir Thomas circled the room in disbelief. "The king hasn't left this room in over twenty years. Where the hell is he hiding?"

He grabbed Sydney's arm again. "Come with me. I bet

they moved to the other side of the building to get away from the smoke."

Sir Thomas dragged Sydney through the building, checking every room while growing more and more agitated.

A sense of delight grew in Sydney at each empty room until she felt almost dizzy with giddiness. The king and Jordan had escaped. She wanted to laugh out loud, but the thunderous expression on Sir Thomas's face stopped her.

"They must be on the next floor down. Hurry up." Sir Thomas grabbed Sydney's arm and nearly pulled her off her feet.

A search of the lower floor revealed more empty rooms. Sydney was happy to see that Sir Lewis and Clark was not in his room. She hoped he had sought safety with the others.

Sir Thomas gave a savage yowl of frustration and grabbed her arm again. He turned and ran for the stairwell.

Sydney lost her balance and fell to her knees, but her captor didn't wait for her to get up. He dragged her behind him until Sydney thought she would scream from the pain in her shoulders.

When they reached the stairwell and Sydney realized Sir Thomas meant to drag her down the stairs she yelled at him to wait. For a moment she thought he couldn't hear her through his anger, but he huffed a short breath and hauled her to her feet again.

Sir Thomas stuck his face in hers. "Stay on your feet. I'll have to kill you now if you're going to keep slowing me down. Understand?"

His sour breath gagged her but Sydney managed to hide her revulsion and nod. She had no doubt he would follow through on his threat.

They made it down to the rubble path without further incident. Although the sun's rays weren't high enough to shine through the light hole, soft daylight illuminated the town.

Sir Thomas looked toward the burning buildings and then toward the still standing shanties. "Where have they all gone?" he asked. "It makes no sense. Most of those people haven't left this building since they were committed. They must be in a panic."

He turned in a slow circle and then stilled. "The lake. They've gone to the lake. Come on. I'm going to need a hostage and you seem to be the only one available."

SYDNEY BLINKED. And blinked again. She wanted to rub her eyes to be sure she was seeing what she thought she was seeing.

More than half of the king's court frolicked in the lake in naked splendor. There was no other way to describe it. The others were in the lake as well, their wet clothing clinging to their dancing bodies. Their shouts and laughter sounded more like young children than middle-aged adults.

The town was burning down around their ears and they were splashing and laughing and chasing one another like a group of innocents without a care in the world. Sydney wanted to laugh out loud. She giggled and earned a nasty glare from Sir Thomas.

Given the pungent body odor in the king's chambers, Sydney thought this might be the first time the patient's bodies had touched water since they fell into the sinkhole. She wished she had bars of soap to pass around.

An urge to join the playful group overwhelmed her. She wanted to splash in the clear water, wanted to wash the smell of smoke from her hair and skin. Most of all she wanted to swim and float and feel the water's silky coolness caress her body. When was the last time she had done something for the sheer joy of it?

She thought back. She hadn't indulged in simple fun since the day of her sister Shannon's murder when she had been idling an afternoon away in the loft of her grandfather's barn. The memory brought the seriousness of the present situation crashing back.

As if reading her mind, Sir Thomas tightened his grip on her arm.

Sydney searched the shore for Jordan and found him standing next to the king with Silas. All three looked okay, unharmed. A small sigh of relief escaped her lips.

Sir Thomas pulled her to a stop. He squinted at Silas and Sydney realized that he didn't recognize the boy he had once tried to kill with fire. Silas's unblemished side faced them. Sir Thomas saw only a tall, handsome stranger standing beside the king.

"Who is that with the king?" hissed Sir Thomas. "Where did he come from?"

Sydney shrugged. She was enjoying Sir Thomas's confusion. "I have no idea," she replied. "Are you sure he's not one of the patients?"

Sir Thomas stood very still and stared hard at Silas. He frowned and shook his head slightly. "He's not one of the patients. I know them all. Perhaps Sir William found him wandering the cavern."

He continued to stare at Silas. "But there's something. Something familiar about him. Well, it makes no matter. I'll deal with him easily enough." Smug certainty rang in his voice.

Sir Thomas is done for, thought Sydney. He can't possibly overpower Silas and Jordan. Her relief was short-lived, however. Sir Thomas pulled her crossbow from his shoulder and nocked a bolt.

"That's only a pistol, Sir Thomas." She forced a heavy scoff into her voice. She knew Sir Thomas had a large ego and wouldn't care for her tone. She wanted him to keep his focus on her, not Silas.

"Unlike a regular crossbow that can strike a target several hundred yards away, it's good for short-range shooting only. You have to get much closer with a pistol if you want to inflict damage."

"I know that. Do you think I'm stupid?" Sir Thomas grabbed her arm again and led her forward.

Sydney wished Silas would turn his head and spot them. As if hearing her thoughts, Jordan turned and looked right at her. She knew they had drawn close enough for him to see her aura, knew he would recognize her clear light.

She watched Jordan speak to Silas. Silas turned and looked at them, still keeping his disfigured side away from their view.

Sir Thomas stopped. "Who is that?" he asked again. Sydney could hear uncertainty and the beginnings of doubt in his voice. She hid a smile.

"Are you sure you don't know him, Sir Thomas? He looks as if he knows you." It was stupid to goad Sir Thomas. She knew this, but she couldn't help herself.

Sir Thomas stared hard at Silas, then he gasped. He shook his head. "Can't be," he muttered. "I'm sure he's dead."

Sydney felt the hand holding her arm tremble. That was a good thing. The more off-kilter Sir Thomas became the easier it would be to subdue him.

"Can't be who, Sir Thomas? Who is dead?" she whispered, feigning innocence.

"No one. I told you, he's dead. It's just someone who reminds me of him, that's all." Sir Thomas nodded his head. "That's all it is," he repeated. "He reminds me of someone."

Sydney turned her head and looked into her captor's eyes. His brow was wrinkled, his eyes worried. She decided to push him some more.

"Who is dead, Sir Thomas?" she asked, louder this time.

Sir Thomas's hand tightened further on Sydney's arm and he shook her. "Stop talking. I need to think."

"Who, Sir Thomas?" Demanded Sydney, nearly shouting now. "WHO does that man remind you of?"

"I said, STOP TALKING." Sir Thomas gave Sydney a hard shake. She clamped her jaw tight to keep from biting her tongue.

The patients in the lake heard Sir Thomas shout. They stopped mid-frolic and stared at the shore. The quiet hiss and pop of the dying fires broke the sudden silence.

Sir Thomas lifted the crossbow and aimed it at Silas. "You're dead. Who are you? What are you doing here?"

"I'm here to help my friend, Elvis," answered Silas in his harsh whisper. He turned and faced Sir Thomas full-on. "Obviously I'm not dead." Silas waited for Sir Thomas to recognize him.

"You! I don't believe it. You were in the hospital with burns over fifty percent of your body. How did you survive? You're supposed to be dead, damn you."

Silas's mouth spread into a lopsided smile. "Sorry about that. I had to live so I could pay you back. The thought of revenge got me through the years and pain of healing."

Sir Thomas leaned forward. "You suffered, huh? I always

wondered what the creatures I set on fire felt. Tell me about it."

Silas's expression turned grim. "I'd much rather help you experience it for yourself, brother. My father always used to say there's nothing like firsthand knowledge."

Sir Thomas scoffed and aimed the crossbow at Silas's chest. "Enough of this bullshit. Move away from the king, Silas. You too, Sir Jordan. The king dies first, then his minstrel."

His lips thinned into a humorless grin. "I'll save you for last, brother. It will give me a great deal of pleasure to finish the job I started more than twenty years ago."

Nobody moved. Silas stayed by the king's side and stared silently at Sir Thomas. Jordan stood on the king's other side and stared at Sydney. She kept her eyes on Jordan but her awareness remained centered on the crazy man holding her hostage. Her nerves felt as taut as the drawn bowstring.

Sir Thomas gave a mean chuckle. "If you don't do as I say I will kill this little lady first. And I know none of you want to see that happen. She's such a pretty little thing."

Silas and Jordan reluctantly took one step away from the king. Sir Thomas shifted the crossbow to the king's massive chest. "This is it, Your Highness. I'm done listening to you talk in song titles. It was entertaining at first, but after twenty years it makes me want to pull my hair out."

The king looked back at Sir Thomas, head held high. "Fool. You're The Devil In Disguise. You Better Run."

Sir Thomas barked a laugh. "That's rich. A chair bound fatso telling me I better run." He moved the crossbow from the king's chest to his loincloth. "How are you gonna stop me, your majesty? Sing me into submission?" He laughed at his own joke, a humorless, ugly sound.

Sydney's entire being focused on Sir Thomas's trigger

finger. She saw its tiny muscles begin to tighten and knew she couldn't wait any longer. She sagged and let all her weight hang from Sir Thomas's hand. Her bound arms jerked back and up. She bit her lip to keep from crying out and prayed that she hadn't dislocated her own shoulder.

Sir Thomas swore and let go of her bicep. With a quick, sharp movement Sydney straightened her knees and drove her shoulder into his side. To her dismay, Sir Thomas staggered but kept his balance. She heard the crossbow string twang and prayed the bolt wouldn't hit anyone.

Sir Thomas cursed and flung the crossbow aside. He pushed Sydney away and ran toward Silas. "You bastard," he screamed. "You've ruined everything."

Sydney stumbled but managed to catch herself before she fell. She ran awkwardly after Sir Thomas, despite the fact there was little she could do with her hands tied behind her back. She'd be damned before she let him hurt Silas any more than he already had.

"Get Back," commanded the king.

Sir Thomas ignored him. He leaped onto Silas, knocking him to the ground. Silas's head hit a rock and he lost his grip on his cane. He lay under Sir Thomas, stunned.

Sir Thomas picked up the cane, looked at it, and flung it back to the ground. He groped for another rock and lifted it high over his head, an ugly smirk on his face. "I guess it's going to come out all right after all," he said, and smiled.

"Silas, get up," screamed Sydney. Panic seized her as she realized she wasn't going to reach the two men in time to stop Sir Thomas from bashing Silas with the rock. "Silas! Don't let the bastard win."

Jordan groped for the king's chair and began to move around it. He felt the same helplessness and inadequacy that he had experienced when he first went blind. The tension made him feel sick to his stomach.

He knew that Sydney was in danger and there was nothing he could do to help her. The auras beside the king were flaring brilliant red and he'd lost track of who was who.

He'd never felt so helpless or so afraid. If anything happened to Sydney…he forced the thought from his mind.

The king flung out an arm and stopped Jordan. "Get Back." He leaned down and picked up Silas's cane with his other hand. With a quick movement he unsheathed the hidden sword and drove it into Sir Thomas's back.

Sir Thomas turned and looked at the king, his mouth hung open with surprise; then he dropped the stone and fell forward.

"For Ol' Times Sake," said the king. He leaned down and pulled the sword from Sir Thomas's back, wiped it on the dead man's shirt, and stuck it back into the cane.

Sydney stumbled over to Jordan and turned her back to him. "Please untie me."

Jordan smiled and grasped her by the shoulders. He ran his hands down her arms until he felt the plastic tie, wincing when he felt the slick blood on her wrists. He pulled on it but it was too strong to break with his bare hands.

"Where's your knife? I'll have to cut the tie."

"Sir Thomas took it." Sydney turned to look at Sir Thomas. The sun had risen high enough to penetrate the sinkhole. Rays of sunlight made the fresh blood covering Silas's clothing shine. Her stomach roiled. She swallowed and hastily looked away.

"Is he-is he dead?"

Silas groaned and pushed Sir Thomas's body to the side. He hesitated, then wiped his bloody hands on the dead man's pants.

"Yes. He's very dead," he answered. Silas felt Sir Thomas's pockets and found Sydney's knife. He handed it up to the king who placed it into Jordan's hand.

Jordan hesitated. What if he cut Sydney instead? He knew she kept her blade ultra-sharp. It would be so easy to miss and nick her instead. He handed the knife back to the king.

"The king had better do this, Syd. I might miss."

The king cut the tie from Sydney's wrists and Jordan brought them around to her front. He gently rubbed her hands to get the circulation moving in her fingers while she gingerly rolled and stretched her shoulders.

Sydney took a step away and Jordan grabbed her around the waist and brought her close.

"Don't ever scare me like that again," he whispered into her ear. "I was beyond panic at the thought of losing you."

"Afraid you'll have to find a new caretaker?" she teased.

"To be honest, I was afraid you might think about running off with your new friend Silas. Angeline says he's very handsome." Jordan kept his tone light, disguising the fact that he was serious. Why would a woman like Sydney choose to be with a handicapped man when she could do much better?

"Angeline's right," agreed Sydney. "Silas is very handsome. And smart. And interesting." She watched Jordan's expression tighten and decided to stop teasing him.

"But he's not you." She stood on tiptoe and brushed his lips lightly with her own. "You can't get rid of me that easily," she said.

Jordan's arms tightened around her. He hesitated a moment, then kissed her back, a deep, searching kiss that revealed just how much he cared. He held nothing back, and to his relief, Sydney responded. When they broke the kiss off they were both panting.

"Harumph." Silas cleared his throat and coughed.

Sydney grinned at Silas and stepped out of Jordan's arms, much to his dismay. He felt better when she wrapped her arm around his waist and leaned against him. He put an arm around her shoulders and planted a kiss on top of her head. Underneath the smoke she still smelled of the spicy fresh aroma that was uniquely hers.

Silas looked at the king and smiled his half-smile. "Thank you, your majesty. You saved my life," he rasped.

"My Heart Cries For You. Such A Night. There's A Brand New Day On The Horizon."

"No need to cry for me, Elvis. I manage okay. I'm happy to see you looking so well. It's been far too long," replied Silas.

"Funny How Time Slips Away," said the king.

Silas hesitated a moment, then took off his bloody shirt, exposing the ugly burn scars that covered half his chest and one arm. "Sorry to expose you folks to my ugliness," he said quietly, "but I can't wear that bloody shirt another moment. Excuse me while I go clean up." He went down to the lake and dove into the water.

"What did he mean by his ugliness?" asked Jordan. "I thought you said Silas was handsome?"

"He is handsome. Devastatingly handsome. He also has second and third degree burn scars over half of his face and body," Sydney replied. "Sir Thomas tied Silas to his bed and set it on fire. Fortunately Silas's father smelled the smoke and found him before it killed him."

Jordan shook his head. People could be so messed up. "Sir Thomas mentioned setting fire to his adopted brother. Poor Silas."

"Sir Thomas was actually the adopted one, not Silas," Sydney corrected. "Thomas burned down his own family's house with his parents asleep in their bed. He murdered his natural mother and father, but no one learned the truth until it was too late. His mother and Silas's mother were sisters so Silas's parents adopted Thomas when he was orphaned. Then he tried to kill Silas with fire."

"That explains Silas's aura," said Jordan. "I wondered why it flares tall on one side and is almost nonexistent on the other." He took his arm from Sydney's shoulders and began to unbutton his shirt.

"What are you doing?"

Jordan shrugged out of the shirt. "I have a feeling Silas needs this more than I do. I'm sure he won't want to parade his scars around in front of all these strangers."

Sydney stretched up and kissed him under the jaw. "My hero. Not only brave but sensitive. No wonder I love you."

Jordan stilled. Did Sydney just say that she loved him? Or was it just an expression that meant nothing?

Before he could pursue the subject Silas returned.

"What should we do with Sir Thomas's body?" asked Sydney.

Silas thanked Jordan for the shirt. He frowned as he used it to dry his torso, then put it on.

"We can't bury him down here and we can't throw him in the lake—the body would pollute their drinking water."

He looked back at what was left of the town. "We could toss him onto one of those piles of coals and toss some fresh wood on it, like a funeral pyre. That seems fitting, don't you agree? Jordan, give me hand with the body, would you please?"

A short time later the burnt shanty next to the asylum flared into flames again and Sir Thomas became one with his obsession. The king's court danced around the burning body while the king sang "Amazing Grace" followed by "You Ain't Nothing But A Hound Dog."

Even Sydney and Jordan danced with Dogma standing close by, and eventually Angeline grabbed Silas and pulled him into the fray.

I 4

THE KING'S followers definitely smell much sweeter these days, thought Sydney as she watched Elvis's court gather around their leader. They were back out by the lake after several restful nights sleeping in the asylum.

Now that the taboo of leaving the building had been broken, everyone wanted to come outside. A constant stream of inmates flowed between the asylum and the lake. They had even widened the rubble path to ease their way. Sydney considered their new activity a positive sign and hoped for their sakes it indicated improved mental stability.

Sir Henry and Angeline had made several trips to the surface with Sydney and Silas, bringing clothing, soap, and food to share with the others.

Silas had tried to persuade the inmates to move to the surface, but they wouldn't leave the familiar security of the brick asylum they called home.

Silas gave the king his father's gold-headed cane in appreciation for saving his life. Much to Jordan's relief, the ram's head staff was found and the king returned it to Jordan.

On the third day after Sir Thomas's death, Angeline asked

Silas to marry her. He said yes and the king offered to perform the service.

Sydney stood on Angeline's left as the maid of honor. The entire female population of the asylum, plus one confused male, had insisted that they be allowed to participate as bridesmaids.

Sydney had scoured the town of Farmington and found a wedding gown that fit Angeline and a silky red dress that fit her own body like a second skin.

It felt strange to wear a fancy dress after several years dressed only in jeans and camouflage pants. Sydney found herself fingering the short hem of her dress while she stood next to the bride. A part of her, the part that still cared about such things, wished Jordan could see her in the dress.

The other bridesmaids were dressed in an odd mishmash of skirts, dresses, and high heels. All wore bright red lipstick smeared across their lips, even the lone male. They would have fit into any clown circus, thought Sydney, smiling at their excited faces.

She looked across Angeline and beyond Silas, to where Jordan and Dogma stood at Silas's side. Jordan had graciously agreed to be Silas's best man. Both men looked resplendent in their tuxedos and Sydney was reminded of the fact that at one time tuxedos were a way of life for Jordan.

Behind them the men of Graceville stood at stiff attention. She averted her gaze from the ones who had refused to don their clothes after romping in the lake.

She turned her attention to the king's throne and waited for the ceremony to begin. The king had draped himself in a metallic gold curtain, toga style, for the occasion. With his gold-headed cane he looked like a comic book king.

"Sweet Angeline. Anyone Could Fall In Love With You," began the king.

Oh, no, thought Sydney. How on earth is the king going to manage this with song titles?

"Dearly beloved, we are gathered here today," the king continued, and Sydney's jaw dropped. The king smiled and winked at her. "It's near impossible to marry them properly using only song titles," he said.

She grinned back and the ceremony continued on without a hitch. When the bride and groom said their "I dos" the king's court echoed their promise.

"Dooo, dooo," they chanted. Sydney found herself laughing. She hadn't felt this lighthearted since before the upheaval. She could almost forget all the terrible things that had happened and believe that everything was going to be all right again.

Later that evening everyone gathered around a bonfire that had been built earlier on the lake shore. Silas brought his guitar, Sir Henry and another man used buckets to beat a rhythm, and the king sang song after song.

"May I have this dance?" Jordan stood at Sydney's shoulder.

She turned into him and he wrapped an arm around her waist and held her hand on his chest with the other. She lifted her free hand and placed it lightly around his neck, bringing her body closer.

She felt his hand slide up her bare back and stop. He stood very still.

"Holy cow, what are you wearing?"

"It's a sexy little backless number. Fire truck red. Looks great with my dark hair. I thought you might like it," she replied.

"I love it." He slid his hand down and cupped her, pulling

her even closer. The dress felt cool and slinky over Sydney's round, firm bottom.

"But I'm insanely jealous that everyone but me gets to see you in it."

Sydney laid her cheek on his chest. "That's true," she said softly, "but you are the only one I will dance with, so no one but you will feel it on my body."

He slid his hand slowly up Sydney's back, relishing her smooth skin. I need this woman in my life, he thought. I love her more than life. I'm so lucky she wandered into my yard that day.

He lifted his hand and cupped the back of her head and kissed her mouth with soft lips.

Sydney responded and he deepened the kiss, sliding his tongue along her full lower lip. She sighed and leaned into him and he kissed her harder, letting her feel his need. She wrapped her arms around his neck and pressed her body to his until he thought he'd burst into flame from the heat.

Sir Henry waltzed by and whistled.

Shocked by the intensity of her feelings, Sydney pulled back. She dropped her arms and pressed her hands against Jordan's chest.

She couldn't do this. It wasn't fair to Jordan. He didn't know anything about the heavy weight of guilt she carried. She wasn't the woman he thought she was.

"I don't understand," he said, confused and frustrated by her withdrawal. "We obviously care for each other. Why won't you let our relationship follow its natural course?"

"I can't," whispered Sydney. "There are things you don't know about me…"

Jordan felt for and grabbed both her hands to keep her from bolting. "Then tell me. I can help you with these things, whatever they are. Talk to me, sweetheart. Let me help you. Please."

"I can't." Sydney shook her head. This was too hard. She wanted Jordan, knew that she loved him, wanted to feel free to accept his love in return. She took a deep, shuddering breath.

"Trust me, you won't feel the same about me after you know the truth. I'm not to be trusted. I'll let you down when you need me most."

She pulled her hands free. "I'm going to bed. We're leaving early tomorrow and I need to rest."

She turned and hurried off before Jordan could stop her. She wanted to tell him. She wanted to share her pain and guilt and have him hold her and tell her that there had been nothing she could do to save her sister.

She desperately wanted to hear him say that he loved her anyway.

She sighed. She couldn't do it. Smokey was the only one she trusted to hear her confession. Smokey would tell her whether she was fit to love or not. In the meantime it was wrong to lead Jordan on, wrong to give him hope for a future with her.

Tears gathered in her eyes. Sometimes life plain old sucked.

***

Sydney was eager to leave Graceville but she dreaded heading back into the inky blackness of the aquifer and it made her cranky. How long would it would be before she saw the sky and sunshine again?

She sighed and turned to Jordan standing silently beside her. "I have to find Sir Lewie and say goodbye," she said.

"Who's Sir Lewie? I don't remember meeting him," said Jordan, feeling rather cranky himself. He was ready to go, eager to be alone with Sydney again and have another opportunity to break through the wall she kept erecting between them. He reached down and scratched Dogma between her ears to hide his scowl.

"Sir Lewis and Clark," said Sydney. "I told you about him. He wants to shoot himself out of a canon to the other side of the lake. Wait here. I'm going to check the lake to see if he's down there."

She hurried off before Jordan could dissuade her. She didn't know why she couldn't just tell Jordan that she was terrified to go into the darkness again.

Maybe because he lives in darkness all the time and my fear of it makes me feel petty and unworthy.

The thought caught her by surprise.

She found half a dozen patients frolicking in the lake but no Sir Lewis and Clark. When she asked if anyone had seen him they pointed to the water tower. Its rainbow-striped form sat fifty feet from the shore, the broken support column jutting up from the tank like the bridge of a submarine.

"Lewie! Sir Lewis and Clark! Where are you?" She waited a moment, then turned to go. A shout made her turn back. She scouted the people in the lake but didn't see the wannabe explorer.

"Christmas Ghost! Ahoy! Up here."

Sydney looked at the water tower and realized someone was waving to her from the broken support column. She laughed and waved back.

"Sir Lewie, what are you doing?" she called out.

"This is better than a canon, Christmas Ghost. I can explore in comfort from this ship. Thank you for keeping your promise. Maybe I'll see you in my travels."

Sydney waved good-bye and headed back toward the hospital. Several of the men were clearing away the debris from the burned shanties, preparing to rebuild. The extra light from the enlarged sinkhole had created more gardening space and Angeline and Silas were organizing workers to tend the food plots.

Silas saw her and excused himself from the group.

"Hey," he said when he caught up to her. "Are you and Jordan ready to leave?"

"I guess," said Sydney. "I mean, sure, yes, we're headed out."

Silas placed a hand on Sydney's arm. She looked up into his face and smiled. He looked so happy, not like the vengeful man she had met only a few days ago.

"What's wrong, Sydney?" he asked. "Would you rather stay? You and Jordan are welcome here, you know."

She shook her head. "No, it's not that. We have to go. It's just—it's the dark, Silas. I don't want to be underground any more. I hate it. And I feel so guilty because Jordan lives his entire life in the dark and I know it's not fair and—"

Silas squeezed her arm. "I think I can help you out. Come with me."

Two hours later, after sharing tearful farewells with the king, Sydney stood on the surface with Jordan, Dogma, Silas, and the chickens. Dogma was still sulking over the indignity of being hauled up through the access hole tied into a bed sheet.

"Are you sure, Silas? What if you need this?"

"I have everything I need right here now that I have Angeline," answered Silas. "Take it with my blessings. Head due west. That will be the fastest way out of here. You should have enough gas to reach the mountains, or at least get within easy hiking distance of them."

Sydney put her pack in the back of the small utility vehicle next to Jordan's bag and the water and gas jugs Silas had filled for them. She secured the hen cages and helped Dogma up, then slid behind the driver's wheel.

"I'm not going to argue," she said. "This will save us days of walking. Thank you. I hope we meet up again one day."

Silas walked back to Jordan.

Jordan reached out a hand and Silas grasped it. "Thanks for everything, Silas. I owe you my life. If I can ever do anything for you don't hesitate to ask."

"Just take good care of Sydney," rasped Silas. "That's all I ask. She helped me when I had nothing left to live for. She changed all that. I owe her my life."

"Yeah, she saved mine too. I'll do my best. We'll be sure to stop by and check on you all if we come back this way."

Jordan ran his hand along the side of the vehicle and guided himself to the front seat. He climbed in and placed his arm across the seat backs and touched Sydney's shoulder.

He had had a lot of time to think last night after Sydney had left him and he'd decided to stop pressuring her. At least until they caught up with her friend Smokey, he amended. After that all bets were off. He intended to marry her if she'd have him, but he'd wait to ask her until she completed her quest to find the mysterious Smokey.

"I hope you know how to drive this thing," he said aloud in a teasing tone. "Ready? Forward ho!"

Sydney smiled and put the vehicle in gear. Soon Nebraska would be behind them. She was one state closer to absolution.

I'm glad you found this book out of the millions available. If you'd like to know what else I've written or when I release a new book instead of leaving it to chance, you can sign up for my newsletter or send me an email through my website CharleyMarshBooks.com. I love to hear from my readers.

And if you want to know what I'm up to on a more regular basis you can follow me on Facebook. https://www.facebook.com/charley.marsh.372

AFTERWORD

Elvis Presley, the real King, was a one of a kind phenomenon. Despite his lack of formal musical training and his inability to read music, his rockabilly style changed the music scene forever.

As of today, Presley still holds the world record as best-selling solo artist. According to Wikipedia, his original master recordings total between 650 and 711 songs, depending on who is counting.

I came across a list of four hundred of Presley's song titles and my character the asylum king was born. Writing a character who speaks only in song titles was challenging but a great deal of fun. I will never repeat it though. Like the original Elvis, my Elvis is one of a kind.

ABOUT THE AUTHOR

In my younger days my curiosity drove me to climb mountains, canoe rivers, and explore caves and wilderness areas from Maine to California. I've been shot at, caught in a desert flash flood, and almost drowned off the Maine coast. Once I tobogganed down a 5,000+ foot mountain.

Life is always an adventure if you have the right attitude.

I never set out to be a storyteller, but looking back on the elaborate lies I made up as a troubled teen I can see that I always had the makings. Now, in the immortal words of Lawrence Block, I happily "make up lies for fun and profit."

If you would like information regarding my new releases or simply want to contact me visit: https:// charleymarshbooks.com/ I am always happy to hear from my readers.

www.ingramcontent.com/pod-product-compliance
Lightning Source LLC
Chambersburg PA
CBHW032027180726
48284CB00008B/2510